CHAPTER 1

IT WAS AS HOT AS PAUL IMAGINED ONE HUNDRED Julys experienced in one giant wave would feel like as 358 3rd Battalion, 5th Marine landed in Da Nang, Vietnam. The intensity of this heat slapped you, hugged you tight then squeezed all the energy out of you. The humidity was a cloak of suffocation giving the day a foreboding gloom that sapped any physical advantage a soldier might have in this jungle.

This was the first time Paul had really felt that enlisting in the Marine Corps might not have been such a great idea. What had drawn him to the Marines was their renowned discipline training. He had thought, with a greater sense of discipline he would find more strength to follow through with the decisions he was making for his future, his life.

So here he was, in Vietnam. After Da Nang, they were to move on to Recon Extract, Quang Tri Province, and that was his future as far as he knew it. On the ASVAB he had scored exceptionally high in the field of medicine, and so he was to be assigned to the medical unit. Another cause for anxiety.

His high school career advisor Mrs. Cattell had said, "Paul, I would not be helping you if I advised you to pursue a medical degree. Negro students have not done well with pre-med courses. Maybe you should consider becoming an attorney like your father, or even an entertainer. Your smile always reminds me of Sammy Davis Jr.!"

But the Armed Services Vocational Aptitude Battery had shown otherwise. And now the jungle would decide who was right or wrong by throwing the challenge of medicine straight at him, in this sink or swim situation.

As Paul focused on the soldiers leaving Da Nang, he noticed their body language. Paul blended in all too well with the majority of men he observed, but something was different with these particular soldiers. They seemed flat, with no emotion, like zombie warriors who had given their all to a futile contest that had ended in a tied score. But there was one man he definitely recognized - Hell, how could you miss him? Freddy Hawkins was six foot seven inches tall wearing all his gear on his back and carrying two duffle bags.

Paul hadn't seen Freddy since he got kicked out of sixth grade - kicked out because he'd come to Paul's rescue when several players from the other team had jumped him after losing the City Basketball Championship, a game where Paul had shot out the lights. He'd tried to explain the circumstances to the nuns but apparently it was some kind of final straw for Freddy. Reverend Mother Mary Catherine wouldn't budge on her decision to expel him from the school.

"Freddy! Freddy! Say, Blood, it's me, Paul Marshall!"

Freddy glanced over with no expression at first. Then a very strange sort of smile crossed his face. "Well, well, if it ain't Captain America. What in the hell is a Bonafide Boojwah like you doin' in a place like this?"

Paul wasn't sure how to respond. He felt guilty for some reason, then angry about feeling guilty, then just at a loss for words.

Freddy glanced around, then locked Paul eye-to-eye and said, "Look Man, they put folks in the Recon Unit for two reasons. Either they feel you're the best of the rest or it was this instead of prison. And criminals without a conscience serve *the dark side*. No mercy, no fear, just the task at hand. Show the enemy this is serious shit."

He looked Paul up and down, as though to measure the 'new' man.

"You must be here 'cause you impressed the Brass. We're the Point Men, the eyes for the next move on the chess board. But get this - some of your Brother Soldiers may not want you to survive this place. Understand? To them, the Enemy is whatever gets seeded in their already damaged minds."

Paul was taken aback. The intensity coming off his old friend seemed as fierce as the heat.

"It's *Play or Die* time, Blood. You a part of both worlds now. The White World 'cause of your smarts and the Black 'cause of your skin. No time to continue your education, so think careful on what I just told you. And know I still got your back."

"I appreciate that," Paul said.

Freddy's eyes softened. "Look Man, I want you to check out a friend of mine; he'll probably be at the base you're heading to. He's the medic on the team. You goin' to Quad Sui?"

"Yeah," Paul said, "How'd you know?"

"Educated guess," Freddy smiled. "Look for Eddy Harris, Sergeant Harris. Tell him we Homeboys and he'll be your Guardian Angel."

At last Freddy flashed a genuine smile as he placed his hand on Paul's shoulder.

"Just like that night when I saved yo ass from those honkies."

Freddy shook Paul's shoulder as both men laughed.

"I gotta go now but Watch Out; it's a different world here. *Not everyone plans on you going home.*"

As Freddy walked away, Paul thought of a half dozen questions he wished he'd asked. Like where did Freddy go after leaving their little parochial school? And was he one of those who had been given the option of *Jail or War?*

That first night in the barracks, Paul's ongoing battle with insomnia was compounded by the heat. He hadn't had a decent night's sleep since he'd decided to enlist. Now, between swatting insects and the intense humidity, every time he closed his eyes he saw JoAnn. Was he running away from her or running back to her? His plan to become a Marine was supposed to allow him the time and space to piece their lives together, see what their future would look like. Where he might have messed up was not talking about it with her before he decided to split from their lives in San Francisco.

But enough of that. It was time to gather up all those feelings and get them back in the box with the lid firmly in place. This was Vietnam. Now the focus was *STAYING ALIVE*.

CHAPTER 2

THE FOLLOWING WEEK, WHILE PAUL WAS SITTING IN the PX, his Commanding Officer sat down next to him. The two Brothers sitting at his table got up and moved to another. Major John Wilson Larson's stern, angular face matched his reputation as a tough World War II vet.

"I have a job for you," he said, then suddenly stood right back up and walked out of the room. Paul got up and followed.

The Major's office was small and hot with no ceiling fan. His desk was stacked with neatly laid out papers and files.

"Have a seat," he said as Paul entered. "You haven't been here long, have you?"

"Uh, No Sir. Just arrived. Haven't been asked to do much yet."

"Well, what I hear is you've got the making of a great future in the Corps." The Major leafed through a file on his desktop. "Your profile here, words of recommendation." He closed the file and tapped his fingers on the cover. "I understand you've been asking around about a Sergeant Edward Harris. You know this man? You're not from Chicago or related to him in any way. That correct?"

"Yes Sir, he's a friend of a friend, guy I knew in grammar school."

The Major opened the file next to Paul's. "Edward Thomas Harris. Born in Chicago, has a bachelor's degree, spent a year in medical school, got into some trouble with the law. Looks like he was facing an assault and battery deal. You have been assigned to his outfit, the medical corps. He will be your lead man." The Major closed the file. "Well, his situation wasn't as serious as some of your other brother Marines, I guess. All the same, we've got reason to believe there's more to this man's profile. We need more information. I want you to seek out this man and find out everything you can about him. We believe he's involved in some illegal activity but can't pin it on him."

Paul looked deep into the Major's eyes and for some reason they reminded him of Reverend Mother Mary Catherine.

"May I ask why, Sir?" said Paul tentatively. He could imagine that turning snitch after just arriving in this place could only be hazardous to his health.

"Why? Did I hear the word Why? I started this conversation saying you have a future. You're officer material or so I thought. I told you Harris' history and what was required. DISMISSED!"

Paul stood up, saluted, and walked out the door.

Paul had a long talk with himself that night. His future of being promoted to an officer did not concern him as much as the feeling that this man Harris had broken the law before coming to the military. Why else would his Superior Officer be concerned about his current activities? Paul stopped the questions. He had been given an assignment and would carry it out, no matter where it would take him.

The next morning while at breakfast Paul was handed a note.

I'm in the Supply Compound. Inquire there.

Paul made his way to the supply tent. Just inside the entry he pulled an older Marine aside. "I'm looking for a Sergeant Edward T. Harris. You know him?"

The older Marine nodded respectfully. "Yes Sir. Just a second." He craned his neck and called toward the rear of the tent. "Hey Eddie! Some Youngblood over here to see you."

Paul was pointed to a room in the back where Sergeant Harris came strutting forward to greet him. He was a big man, neatly dressed and out of uniform, wearing an embroidered silk shirt with his regulation pants. His smile lit up the room. "Yeah Yeah, how you doing Lil Bro? I been waitin' on you. Freddy dropped me a dime last week you'd be coming around. How'd the talk go with Major Larson?"

Paul was no poker player. His mouth dropped open.

Harris threw up a well-manicured hand with several shiny rings on his fingers. "Gotta get this call, sit over there."

Paul waited out the phone call. When Harris had finished he turned to Paul, serious as a heart attack, and caught him completely off guard. No more smile, just straight up intensity.

"Let me start out by saying I know they want you to be a spy. I know you were with Major Larson and that he ordered you to come over here and report back. Don't be shocked or surprised, my Man. You think you're the first one they sent over here?"

"Look, I don't—"

"Take it easy, Man, take it easy. Just know I got spies too."

Paul could feel the sweat streaming down his back, sticking his shirt to his skin.

"But you know, I thought about you, had myself a look at your file too. Yeah, Brother, let me tell you, I have met many like you, many. How old are you - nineteen, twenty?"

"I thought you said you read my file," Paul said.

"Your age don't make no difference to me, Youngblood. I've met you in all ages, all colors, male and female. And what it is, what the real deal is, I hated you. But I've learned to love all. The circle must remain intact no matter where the attack begins on *the Brotherhood*. It took a lot of searching and thinking and letting shit go that I would *never* have let go before I became a Marine, before I came to 'Nam. But here's the thing - getting assigned as the medic on the team, you become spiritually involved. Not necessarily from a religious side, more from a unity perspective, Dig? In fact, all aspects of life become more important, even the enemy we have to go through to get out of this place. I've seen shit that will stay with me and haunt me the rest of my life. Not anything I did

7

personally, but things I have no way of separating myself from. The village we just trashed. Trying to keep a mutilated brother alive who had been butchered by the Viet Cong. Begging me to end his life right there in the jungle."

He took a second to make sure Paul's eyes met his.

"I love you especially, because we go back a long way. Maybe even the same slave ship brought us over four, five hundred years ago. Maybe we even sold on the same platform two hundred years ago. Our ancestors danced and hugged each other when Lincoln emancipated us. Yeah, we go a long way back. Shit, we may even be from the same tribe, before my family went North and yours went West and others stayed in the South.

"I love you but I hate you. Because education somehow made you less educated, less compassionate to my Father's people. As the gods showered your Grandfather's children with wealth and beautiful homes, others of the Tribe became poorer and poorer. I hate you because you refuse to see our similarities. Same thick lips, same nose, same hair, but you're afraid to make the connection. Can't you see it's self-hatred, Youngblood? You can't hide what's in the mirror."

It was like being back in his high school civics class, like Malcolm X was preaching to the crowd, and Paul hung onto every word. Harris was making a lot of sense, but he wasn't talking about Paul's family. His people had gone to school, studied, and worked hard for their good fortune. Harris was talking about someone else, not him. But he couldn't deny he was squirming uncomfortably in his seat, feeling very defensive.

So without forethought, Paul shot back, "Yeah, Man, that's us. Nothing wrong with living in comfort enjoying what's considered the finer things in life, if you earned it. Like that shirt you've got on, those rings. I can tell you right now, I have no hatred for white people as a race - some good, some bad. Just like black folks - some good, some bad. But it's your kind I don't like. You, Harris. The ones born with the brains and opportunity to be somebody and you blow it up. Man, you were on the way to becoming a doctor when you fucked it up!"

Harris seemed surprised, like he wasn't used to comeback.

"I was rook'd out of that spot. I lost my cool and paid for it. I didn't kill the punk who punk'd me; I threatened to kill his ass and the powers that be, took my threat to the ultimate level - a criminal assault charge. And Yeah, I did land a punch, but I owned my action and was given another chance. I got sent here.

"You think I wasn't talking about you and your people. Well, my Man, that's where you got some growing to do. But take it easy, my Brother, you gonna be alright. I invite you to do what the CO assigned you to do. Watch me, study me, work beside me. Learn some medical skills, something you can use out there on Recon and Extract. Some of us won't make it back. Trust me. I need you more than Major Larson needs you.

"You have a responsibility to your Blackness. You have a debt to pay to your People, our People, our Ancestors. To the Institutions we've already started, the ones that need to be started, to better educate, better prepare those less lucky, less fortunate, but just as deserving. I went to the same White schools as you. Shit gotta change to make Black people more comfortable wherever they choose to learn. But until that day comes, we don't need more jails, more Vietnams. Our world needs help. Serious help. And the Lord put you here to help make that change. But for god sake, ask the tough questions: *Who am I? Am I my own man?*"

Paul made a decision right then and there, the Sarge was no lunatic. This was a serious, stand-up kinda guy. There were things to learn from being in this man's circle.

Time moved quickly from that first meeting. Paul initially kept a running count of people extracted from the battle sites with descriptions of their wounds and treatment. He'd meant to send the tally to JoAnn, but the count eventually got lost and he never mailed any of his letters.

But he did keep talking with Harris.

"Hey Sarge, the thing that gets me is you never know which of the soldiers we're dealing with will live or die. I mean, one Brother looks so fucked up with wounds and shit that he won't make it one more minute, yet he ends up going home. Another guy seems to have a trivial wound and dies right there in your arms."

"That's why you treat 'em all the same. Everyone deserves another day. No matter who they are or what the situation looks like in that moment, *just do your absolute best.*"

"Yeah, at least you sleep better that way." Paul agreed.

"Too many people in our position take on the role of GOD. They make decisions based on statistics from a book they read. Well, I rely on the book *I'm* writing. And since *I'm* still gathering information, there's room for miracles."

This made sense to Paul and he easily adopted this same plan of action as his own.

CHAPTER 3

HIS FIRST TOUR OF DUTY WAS COMING TO THE END and he was considering enlisting for a second. Paul discovered that Harris had helped Freddie get assigned to a top-level platoon in Okinawa where he was receiving special training, something he could carry into civilian life after his tour of duty. Sergeant Harris had been assigned to another unit. Major Larsen, after six months of having Harris shadowed, divulged to Paul that the Sergeant was being considered for a chance to complete his medical degree. Some higher-ups were not on board with the idea, so the information gathering would continue when Harris transferred to the U.S. Naval Hospital on Okinawa. If all went well there he would be given the chance to re-enter medical school back in the States.

Paul was the Medic now and the year had been a bittersweet experience. He'd come to learn that you have to live each day as it presented itself. *Tomorrow was never guaranteed.* Many medical skills had been mastered and he'd found medical jargon an easy pickup as well. A comminuted, displaced fracture was simply a bone broken in many pieces; a soldier having trouble breathing or feeling like they were drowning usually meant a serious injury to their lungs - stuff like that.

Tonight was to be a quick search-and-find assignment. A NATO Peacekeeping Outfit had missed their last two checkpoints and were now considered lost in the jungle. But for Paul there was a feeling of doom written all over this assignment. Several of his men had bad drug issues and another one, a preacher's son, was bona fide crazy, collecting Cong body parts as souvenirs to sell or even worse, just to keep as 'good luck charms.' No luck tonight, though. They had successfully found the unit and were on their way back to the base, when BAM, their vehicle hit a landmine and somehow Paul was thrown clear before the vehicle exploded.

When Paul regained consciousness eleven days later, he found himself lying in a hospital bed. He had tried to clear his head several times before but he just couldn't seem to surface. He had wanted to tell the nurse with the Southern twang who'd hovered over him from time to time that he was okay, but his tongue kept failing him. Several times he'd heard her say, "Come on Soldier…Wake up! Stop lying there like a piece of dry toast."

Now his brain was jumping like rapid fire. He had so many thoughts running around in his head it was hard to follow one to the next. Paul vaguely recalled being in the front seat of a vehicle racing down a dark road and suddenly there was an explosion and then nothing more. No white light, no angels singing. Like sitting in a snow-covered place watching… nothing.

> *My little horse must think it queer*
>
> *To stop without a farmhouse near*
>
> *Between the woods and frozen lake*
>
> *The darkest evening of the year.*

That old poem kept rolling around in Paul's brain like a train clanking down its tracks, moving on without a destination in sight.

> *The woods are lovely, dark and deep,*

But I have promises to keep,

And miles to go before I sleep,

And miles to go before I sleep.

... Robert Frost's classic. He remembers a moment of triumphant relief after memorizing and delivering the poem before his classmates. His Mom and Dad, who were both major political forces in their community as well as throughout the San Francisco Bay Area, were rarely available for little school events like that one. But on that day, both parents were in the audience and afterward they took him for ice cream as a reward for doing so well.

"Son, you made us proud today. Always remember that we want you to be the best player on the team, but also, you must know everything in the textbooks you are studying at a superior level. You understand, Son?" his father had asked him. "Why? Because you are *Our Boy*. You are destined for great things."

Then his brain jumped and Paul came back to Sgt. Harris' question to him: "*Who are YOU? Are you your OWN Man?*"

Funny to be ruminating on a poem about a snow-covered field when you're in a sweltering hot humid jungle. The 85th Evac Hospital in Qu Nhon was the largest military hospital in Vietnam, but it was not like hospitals back home in the States. Instead, the hospital was a series of Quonset huts laid out to receive jacked up soldiers being dropped off by helicopters and ambulances from every direction.

"We are the Lucky Ones!" This was a kid his unit had saved. The Canadian trooper lying in the bed next to him fit that phrase into every other sentence as he talked seemingly nonstop throughout the day. He talked about his family in a place called British Columbia, about his favorite hockey team, and about how different Canadians were from most of the jerks he met from the U.S. One minute he would be bragging about how awesome and powerful his country was and in the very next sentence talking about how fucked up it was.

We are the lucky ones. Paul would drown out all other thoughts. He had heard that phrase all his life from his parents, from the nuns who had taught him in elementary school and from his one and only sweetheart, JoAnn. He knew he was blessed to not have been born into a poor family with some sort of illness like Sickle Cell or Polio.

"Hey, Canada's not at war with the Viet Cong? We were told there was a Unit out here that needed help. I can't remember the rest." The kid just kept on talking. "No, we're not at war, we're with NATO as Peacekeepers, 'Monitoring the movement of refugees,' they tell us. Don't get me wrong; there are Canadians fighting here in Vietnam alongside U.S. soldiers, but they crossed the border and enlisted at Induction Boards in little towns in the States that were kinda lax with checking addresses and IDs. But the question I'm really dying to ask, I mean, the question I been wantin' to ask a Negro soldier is…"

Paul wasted no time in correcting him. "We're *BLACK*. Not Negro, my Man; what's your question?"

"Well, our unit has been seeing a lot of flyers put out by the Viet Cong about this not being *your People's War*. Viet Cong people don't call you niggers or second class citizens. What do you think?"

"Propaganda crap is just that…Crap. That's where I'm at with that stuff. And every soldier, White or Black, just wants to get back home and that means dancin' with the one who's going to get yo ass back home, DIG?"

Yeah, it was hot and humid in this place with flies and insects and the smell of human waste hanging over the area like a great big musty blanket. But *he* still had all four limbs and was scheduled to be discharged home soon. He was told by the medical staff how fortunate he was. Everyone else in the accident had died. But the only thing that he was truly aware of was he was leaving *the War*.

Paul had been warned that rambling jumbled thoughts were part of his brain injury. They could become progressively worse or infinitely improved, but at this time, no one could predict how his mental function would end up. He was simply riding the wave.

"You're coming along real good Kid," had been the nurse's comment every day for the past few weeks. A doctor came by once or twice a week and said the same.

While lying in the hospital those several weeks, Paul had plenty of time to think about returning to his *life before Vietnam*.

The Red Cross supplied magazines for the wounded soldiers who were eager to know what was going on back home in the States. "Should I get in step with the Super Fly Brothers scene in *Jet* magazine, or go Hippie style and become a freewheeling dude like my man Jimi Hendrix?"

"You know you can get as good as me on your guitar."

An imaginary conversation with the master Jimi himself had become a frequent game Paul played to break up the monotony. Dreamstreams of stimulating conversations with Robert Frost, also a native of San Francisco, and of course with his girlfriend JoAnn, had kept Paul's need for mental entertainment rolling since the brain trauma.

Jimi Hendrix returned to chat. "Well, bloke, don't believe all that stuff about me being totally zonked every bloomin' minute. Before the UK, I actually did the Chittlin' Circuit with the Isley Brothers, Little Richard, and all o'them."

Sgt. Harris had hipped Paul to the fact that John Allen Hendrix, from Seattle, had been given the option of jail time for car theft or enlisting in the Army back in 1961. He had chosen the Army but then was abruptly discharged the following year, apparently for Incompatibility Issues, whatever that meant. Paul had actually caught Jimi performing at the Monterey Pop Festival in '67 the year before he himself had enlisted in the Marines.

He truly felt a better appreciation for life, for who he was and just how blessed his life was, scrambled brain or not. He felt gratitude for things he'd taken for granted before he'd enlisted. He had *chosen* to come to Vietnam where so many others had *been dumped* to die. He paused to take a solemn moment for all his fellow soldiers who would never come home.

CHAPTER 4

IT WAS 1970 AND THE WORLD HAD BEEN APTLY christened, A BALL OF CONFUSION by the Temptations. The famed TV announcer for the 20-mule team Borax Soap, spokesman for General Electric and the star in over 50 movies, was starting his second term as Governor of California. He was promising to continue his bold, aggressive political and economic initiatives. He would be chopping down all those so-called liberal benefits left behind by Governor Edmund Brown, directed toward those on welfare. This was only one of many unsettling issues that had brought Paul to his present dissatisfaction with his home state and what was going on throughout America.

The 60s were capped by the assassinations of Bobby Kennedy and Reverend Martin Luther King Jr. These events in turn had catapulted the Black Panther Movement, the embracing of Black Power, and the rise of The Nation of Islam as a positive alternative to religion for the many who felt abandoned by their Baptist and other traditional faiths for People of Color.

"Hey Paul," said fellow soldier Turner Wilson one day, "what's new in the paper today?" Paul had moved from talking to Hendrix to recalling a day back in the Quang Tri Province.

"Here take it; I'm finished with it," he said.

As Paul went to hand him the collection of newspapers he was reading, Turner withdrew a little. What he said next blew Paul's mind.

"I can't read very well." Unprompted, he continued, "I thought it was cool to not attend classes like everyone else. The teachers always looked on us as dumb jocks in classroom situations, but then turned around to applaud and seemingly worship us when we were playing. Whoever's to blame, I'm wishing now someone would have broke it down for me that *life after sports* truly sucks without basic reading skills!"

The real irony of Turner's confession was that he always came off as so articulate and glib. Paul would never have imagined he had a literacy problem.

"Would you like me to read with you?" Paul recalled offering.

Turner's eyes lit up with more enthusiasm than Paul had expected. He moved closer as they discussed not just the meaning of the words but how they were pronounced, what a comma did and different sentence structures.

Sgt. Harris had observed the interaction and hooked Paul up with a little group he had arranged of other guys who were interested in acquiring certain basic skills that had somehow not been captured in their developmental years.

It was not about *Separate but Equal* bullshit. 'What needs to be changed,' Paul thought, 'is a higher level of quality through- out the education system.' In terms of fundamental basics, **all** communities should be granted the educational opportunities required to reach their full potential. Thurgood Marshall had done his thing arguing before the Supreme Court for the victory in Brown v. Board of Education, that landmark case in which the Court had ultimately declared that State laws to establish *separate* public schools for Black students and White students were unconstitutional.

Paul decided he was going to make a change. A lot more brothers like the ones he had helped, were just waiting to be given a chance to learn and grow. There were a hundred reasons why their problems existed, but the bottom line was *illiteracy*. Paul would find the resources to turn their lives in the right direction. Maybe becoming a lawyer was not going to be his contribution. He was enjoying this medical stuff. But what would JoAnn say? Would she go along with a career move away from law?

He then realized that maybe this conflict was the crux of his running away to war. Was becoming a lawyer tied to making his life work with his woman? WOW, he had always thought it was his choice, his life, until Harris had planted the seed of *Are you your own Man?*

Now his goals were becoming clearer. He enjoyed tutoring, but did not see himself as a full time educator. Nor did he see himself a lawyer. Those were legitimate and worthy professions, but he didn't see either as being part of his future. He felt he was going to help in his own way.

Yeah. Paul felt good... really good about himself, for the first time in a long while.

CHAPTER 5

PAUL WAS FLYING BACK HOME. HIS HEAD WOUND had given him a ticket out of *the War*.

The stewardess had been smiling at him every time she walked down the aisle since the Up Up and Away TWA plane had taken off. Well, it was actually Central Airlines. They had the government contract to transport U.S. Troops from Japan – the first stop out of 'Nam, back to the United States. Jubilant soldiers had named it the *FREEDOMBIRD*. Paul sat in an aisle seat scrunching up his six foot four inch body. The stewardess' constant smile made Paul very uncomfortable. He had never thought of himself as a Ladies' Man and really didn't want to be one. 'Nah, that ain't me; my eyes and heart belong to Miss JoAnn.' Smiling to himself again, he felt a warm sensation flow through his body whenever he thought of her.

"Hey soldier, are you from Seattle?" the stewardess asked Paul. She had walked up the aisle from the back of the plane and stood over him holding several newspapers. She was fairly tall for a woman and had beautifully toned legs.

"No, I'm from San Francisco," Paul replied as he shifted himself to look up into her hazel eyes.

"Well, would you like the 'Frisco paper or the Seattle one?"

"That's San Francisco, please," Paul said. "No offense intended, but native San Franciscans prefer its full name over 'Frisco,'" he volunteered in a serious but polite tone. She laughed, showing a mouthful of incredibly white teeth as she handed him the entire Sunday Morning edition.

"I like that, and will remember to address your city by its formal name," she said as she turned to offer a paper to the guy on the other side of the aisle. Paul accepted her reply with his usual good humor. "Feel free to call me if you need anything," she added as she went on to the next row.

Paul turned and tried to look around the guy sitting by the window to catch a glimpse of the view. But the window shade was halfway closed and Paul didn't want to wake his dozing seatmate. Paul sat back in his seat, put his paper on the empty center seat and continued the conversation with the stewardess in his head. 'Thank you very much, kind lady. But as soon as we land in San Francisco, I be callin' my *Girl*. And we be gettin' it back together again! Hopefully for the rest of our lives.'

He saw it all in his mind. He and JoAnn would rent a convertible and drive out to Big Sur. He had so much he wanted to say to her. On the drive along the coast there would be plenty of time to make her understand why he had suddenly enlisted in the U.S. Marines and deployed to Vietnam without discussing it with her. He knew he had hurt her with his unilateral decision, but felt he'd had no choice at the time.

Something had felt wrong about his life and its purpose. His life just did not interest him anymore. Being a student athlete on full scholarship at one of the most prestigious institutions in the country did not matter. His parents had everything money could buy, and his childhood sweetheart had blossomed into a goddess. But something was missing and the only solution he could come up with was going far away to figure it out. He would make it up to her; he knew he could.

Paul picked up the *SF Chronicle* and read the first page. Yes, he was on his way back home. He could hardly believe it himself. It had taken nearly losing everything in a far away jungle for him to finally realize just how blessed his life was.

The paper didn't interest him for long and he drifted off to sleep.

The War had been going so poorly that the San Francisco draft board had been overjoyed to send him off. His stint at Camp Pendleton boot camp was modified to get him into combat as quickly as possible.

He had never considered the consequences of whether he would live or die. Or whether his future children would be raised in the same environment that had granted him Stanford University to be followed by Boalt Hall School of Law and an automatic partnership in his father's firm.

Acceptance in 'Nam was no different than what he been familiar with throughout his life. He was always picked first or second to play on whatever team sport was being organized. His superior athletic skills gave him instant popularity and his musical talent on the guitar added to this.

Paul's sleep and thoughts were interrupted by the same stewardess passing with a food cart. He accepted a Coke, sipped it a little then fell back asleep to his same *dreamstreams*.

How different he'd found living with so many Black Men in such close proximity for the first time in his life. Of course, he was Black as was his family. But he had always been told they were a class above other Blacks. His father's youngest brother, Melvin, was only five years older than Paul and had been like a big brother. 'Niggas ain't worth a damn!' was his favorite saying. He talked more about Blacks being inferior than the majority of White racists did! How wrong Paul felt his uncle had been. These were good men. They'd fought side by side in combat and supported each other in their darkest hours. They deserved more than the serious shit most of them had left behind at home to 'Fight for America.'

And there were so many Brothers who left the War just as they came, illiterate and uneducated, only now saddled with other problems…drugs, anger issues, and hopelessness. Mentally healthy vets were an illusion. How could one stay mentally together after surviving the perils of War? Those memories stood out the most as Paul rummaged through what he was leaving, besides *the War*.

Paul woke up again, this time startled by gunfire. He sat up straight in his seat. It only took a second for him to realize he was sitting out of harm's way on an airplane that was moving through the turbulence of a thunderstorm. The attractive stewardess had appeared from nowhere once again, her hands now at his waist as she checked to see if his seatbelt was securely in place. Paul's hands met hers as he looked up and smiled. The stewardess was wearing perfume that smelled just like a flower he had discovered while in the jungle. It lingered in his nostrils. It enhanced all he was feeling inside that was good.

The San Francisco Chronicle was resting on his chest. He rubbed his eyes of the remaining sleep and opened the paper. As he thumbed through, a little tired and anxious but optimistic for what lay ahead, he opened the Society Column and immediately noticed the large picture of a radiant, veiled and gowned JoAnn Washington standing next to the Groom, an attorney named John Ellis, who was all smiles. Paul's mouth dropped; his eyes focused solely on the paper in front of him. His heart felt as if it would explode out of his chest. Yes, dropping off all communication with JoAnn had been a major mistake but he had never imagined it could end their relationship! It was only to be a brief diversion that would ultimately make their future the best it was meant to be.

The caption read: 'Mr. and Mrs. Washington happily announce the marriage of their daughter JoAnn Antoinette Washington to John Frederic Ellis.' The words stabbed deep, piercing Paul's insides, radiating to seemingly every corner of his body, paralyzing him, shattering his dreams. *His* JoAnn was married. Married to someone else! His future had just been snatched away from him. JoAnn had been the centerpiece. It was to *her* he was returning. And that disturbed him the most. All of his self-realization had actually only been about pleasing this woman!!

Paul closed the paper, folded it neatly, and tripped off into a dreamless sleep.

He woke up when the pilot announced they were beginning their descent into San Francisco and everyone cheered. But for Paul, the feelings of joy and excitement regarding his future *were gone*. It was almost like his first day in Vietnam when a sense of gloom was all he felt.

They were descending into a grey foggy day outside. Paul anticipated an ugly scene when he announced his change in career plans to his folks. And worst of all, he was again without an alternative plan. The only certainty was that the Marshalls were not going to accept lightly his decision to *not* pursue the profession they had chosen for him.

Enough on that. Time to think about something else.

His mind jumped briefly back to Vietnam. The hardest part was watching the number of young men arriving and dying in Vietnam, the majority of them Black. Paul had read an article about how President Johnson was professing so much interest in helping the Civil Rights Movement, but his preoccupation with the War was obviously affecting the lack of social and economic reform in the Black Communities. It seemed clear to Paul, at least in his part of the war, the greater number of fatalities were Black. And who said Uncle Sam didn't have *ways and means* to keep the Black Race down? Then, if you ran the numbers of how many babies would have been born if so many hadn't died, you clearly have *population control*.

During Paul's stay in the hospital while reading *Life* and other magazines, he'd discovered that the cross burnings, racial insults, and Confederate Flags of his White comrades were not a reflection of uneducated rednecks but rather a straight up representation of the Racial War raging back home in the U.S.

And now, without JoAnn, a life of seeking legal justice for the masses was not his goal. But what would his contribution be? What would his role be, to bring about change? Paul truly felt lost once again. To help change the law was a noble cause. But was it *his* goal or would he be doing it for other reasons?

No, it was about impressing JoAnn and his parents, not about what would give him fulfillment and satisfaction in a life profession. 'That's a real bummer,' he concluded. Where would he start? He knew he could be a positive force. But *how*? The fear of *what next*, his fear of the future, was once again overwhelming. What was it all about? *LIFE?*

After landing, Paul grabbed his duffle bag and stood on American ground for the first time in what seemed like a very long time. He was still without direction, without a plan. It was like nothing had been accomplished in his *Vietnam Detour* and yet deep inside he knew he had grown and become a better man with a greater appreciation for human life. Paul said to himself, 'So the *search* is still on! I am one of the lucky ones. I will find my direction.'

CHAPTER 6

PAUL FOUND A TELEPHONE AND CALLED HIS parents. It was great hearing his mom's voice on the phone.

"Hey Mom, it's Paul! How's the fog today?"

"Paul, is that you? It's so wonderful to hear your voice. I've missed you so much! We've all missed you."

"Yeah, it's me, your one and only child. I missed you all as well. But I felt that going to War was something I had to do, Mom. Say, I'm back Stateside. *The War* is over for me. Don't worry, I'm fine. Everything is intact. The Lord just found a way to get me out of that place." Paul hesitated. "I was going to call JoAnn, until I read the Sunday newspapers," he quipped in a sarcastic tone.

"Well Son, you have only yourself to blame for that one," Mother Marshall responded, never being one to hold back her thoughts. She looked over at the prom and first communion photographs sitting near the phone in the living room. Why her son had decided to get up one day and trash everything she and his father had so carefully planned out and arranged for him, she would never understand.

"Yeah, I shoulda kept in touch, but I didn't. Moving on to today's news."

"Is that Paul?"

Paul heard his father walk into the room and instantly join the conversation. This was the moment Paul had dreaded the most. His mom was forever his constant supporter, except when he had decided to quit Stanford and go to Vietnam. He'd thought he would have more time to plan the conversation before going up against his folks about no longer wanting to become a lawyer.

'Better now than later,' Paul gulped to himself.

"Son, so great to finally hear from you. Are you back home to stay? Don't tell me you decided on another tour of duty?"

"No, that part of my life is over. But, Well, I need some time. I mean the JoAnn marriage thing took me totally by surprise!"

"And what does that have to do with you getting back on the road to completing law school?"

"Dad, I decided that I'm not going to become a lawyer. I know it's not for me. I have got to find out who I am, be my own *man*." Paul couldn't believe what he had just blurted out. The silence was devastating.

"Stick the knife a little deeper!" was his dad's response, his voice rising. "All your life we've groomed and planned for our child to carry on the legacy! Why? We deserve an answer! I thought the War experience would help you understand Life, as it did me while serving in Europe. It ain't all roses and one monkey don't stop the show. Life is precious and it is your responsibility to use what God gave you to make the most of it. I survived some horrible shit during World War II. They pushed us to all the hot spots but the good Lord spared me and kept on gracing me with so many blessings. But now this. How could you be so selfish?"

Paul wanted to further explain the roots of his disillusionment and that his primary interest in becoming a lawyer had always been to please JoAnn and them, not himself. But now was not the time. His father was just too angry. True, except for the literacy help he'd had the opportunity to provide for his fellow soldiers, *the war* experience had been utterly horrific. And yes, he had survived by the grace of God as well.

"Dad, I truly mean no disrespect!"

"Well then, get your ass back in the saddle and get the job done. You were born to be a star attorney!"

"I can't, I need more time," Paul said with more confidence than he felt.

Both of his parents came to the airport to pick him up. No one spoke for several minutes, and then his mother calmly said, "Well, if you are looking for more hearts to stomp on, your cousin Sue is getting married tomorrow and JoAnn is her maid of honor. I'm sure she and your other family members would appreciate your presence, just to know you're alive and intact." His aunt and uncle had been at the house when he'd called and had already commanded his appearance at the wedding.

It was torture seeing JoAnn in the wedding party. How wonderful she looked. The sleek beehive hairdo she frequently wore on special occasions had been replaced with a loose short cropped afro that framed her delicate features. She'd always been tall and long-limbed with unexpectedly large breasts but now there was a very appealing gentle curviness to her body. The body he'd dreamt of on so many nights, seemed so much more womanly since he'd last seen her. At the reception following the ceremony, Paul bided his time and then walked over to JoAnn.

"Say Jo, what's happening?"

She turned away at first and then said, "I'm fine, thank you."

Paul, now very nervously searching for words, half-heartedly said "Uh, still working for that attorney's office downtown?"

JoAnn answered as if this moment had been rehearsed. Her body language did not match the smile that was pasted on her face. "No Paul. I've actually decided to become a lawyer myself. Ironic, isn't it?" Her face changed to more of a defiant look. "Look, I'm very busy right now and you will have to excuse me. I have a few things to do for Sue."

As she walked away, Paul noticed her proud bearing lacked the previous adolescent, carefree look he remembered, that 'I've got it all and know it' air. He remembered more play behind her huge round eyes and dimpled cheeks. Now that youthful aura was replaced by determination and seriousness.

He was the one who'd experienced the ugliness of war and had seen that despair on the faces of the villagers and his brother soldiers. It remained heavy on his heart. He wondered if his friends and family could see it on *his* face. But JoAnn hadn't experienced the war. Then it hit him. For JoAnn, his leaving had been *abandonment* and as deep a cut as any blade could make. They had promised each other so many things for their future together. He wanted to say how very sorry he was, but what difference would it make? Two years had passed.

'What Is... IS!' Paul resolved quietly to himself.

Later, while he was standing at the punch bowl alone, JoAnn tapped him on the shoulder. "Excuse me Mr. Marshall, no, pardon my ignorance, Sgt. Marshall, it is such a pleasure and a surprise to see you here today!" She was holding a glass of champagne and it was obviously not her first. "Well, I will be starting my first year of law school soon. Yes, I've been accepted to Stanford's Program. And you? Are you going to finish your BA?"

He initially thought to turn his back and walk away from what could turn out to be an ugly scene. Instead, he took a deep breath then chose to respond to the emotions they had both bottled up since they last saw each other. "Let's walk outside a minute," Paul said, fighting to contain any response until they were alone. As they reached the veranda and locked eyes for the first time in what seemed to be much longer than it actually was, he said, "Cut the crap Jo - I fucked up, you moved on, and now there will never be an 'us' again. I never fell out of love with you; I just didn't understand where I was going or what I wanted to become, so I had to get far away to figure it out. I just couldn't live with the fact that I was letting you and my parents down."

"And what about *our Life together? Our Love?*" JoAnn said, now furious. "Did you expect that giving me a ring was all you had to do to keep me waiting for you?"

"Ah, knock it off Jo; I don't have to listen to this shit!" He heard himself say it and instantly wished he'd thought of something better than 'shit' as he braced himself for the comeback.

"Shit! You call pulling a totally selfish, ridiculous stunt by running off to a *War* you knew I opposed, Shit? Then you call discussing why you abandoned me after all our years together, SHIT? Well, here's the ring you left me with," she said angrily as she fished it out of her evening bag. "I guess you already know that the one on my finger is live and definitely moving forward. He's not Paul Marshall, but he does love me and I love him. Let's just chalk 'Paul and JoAnn' up to puppy love; we were children.

"But, *you need to know*, the hardest part to forgive is the way you just disappeared on me. Not a word when you left and then nothing, nothing, and more nothing. I just hope if and when you do get it together, you will have enough respect for the woman you have *real love* for to treat her as a trusted friend. Good bye, Paul."

She turned and walked away. As he watched her make her way across the room to her husband, Paul felt a door slide quietly shut in his heart.

Yes, he had truly loved her and he could not explain why he had hurt her - or his parents, for that matter. But he had, and there was no turning back the clock or making things right without denying something deep within himself. He thought about introducing himself to JoAnn's husband. But then again, she was right. They were nothing now. At least he still had precious memories of the times they had shared. Puppy love she'd called it, but it had been real to him all the same. As for his parents, there was no disrespect meant to them either. Like Sgt. Harris had schooled him: "You got to be your own man, *first*. Only then can you face yourself every morning in the mirror and walk on to the next challenge life will bring. *Never be in doubt of who you are and what you believe!*"

That night, while taking JoAnn's pictures out of his wallet, he came across the phone number of the Canadian soldier he'd spent all those weeks in the hospital listening to. That's when he decided to make his way up to Canada to get away for awhile.

CHAPTER 7

IT WAS AN UNEXPECTEDLY LONG TWENTY-THREE-hour bus trip. The officials at the border were really grilling some U.S. citizens regarding the reason for their visit and how long they would be staying. They were looking for draft dodgers. So Paul was amazed when it was his turn to be questioned and the border guard literally waved him through with no hassle.

"Hey, you sure do remind me of my old roommate back in college, Western Washington State, right down the road from here."

The guard was from some place called Prince Rupert and the Brother had taken him on as a 'little brother.' Brotherman had even visited Prince Rupert one spring break and stayed with the family.

The border guard's story confused Paul, as he didn't have the slightest idea where any of the places mentioned were. But he mentally thanked the guy's Black college roommate for making his entry into Canada so easy.

An hour later the bus pulled into the Greyhound Bus Depot on Dunsmuir and Cambie Street. The weather was a lot more agreeable than he'd been told...Canada was supposedly frozen year-round and primarily inhabited by

French-speaking Eskimos! But in actuality, Vancouver was much more like the downtown San Francisco area, not the area of the city where Paul had grown up which was frequently overcast and gray. The sun was shining here and there was green everywhere. He saw grass and trees and flowers, and every few blocks, a park. The air he was breathing felt just right and smelled right too.

Paul had checked into a very nice hotel, the Ritz, a four-block walk from the bus depot. He had kept to himself the first few days, but was liking what he had seen so far. He'd enjoyed walking the clean, friendly streets. Now he was starting to feel the need for some human interaction. Paul had considered calling the Canadian kid he'd met in the hospital, but didn't feel up to being bombarded with the questions and stories he was sure there would be.

Never being one for shyness, Paul approached a man waiting at a bus stop.

"Pardon me, Brother, but I just got into town and I was wonderin'..." Paul was just getting to his question when the man interrupted him and rattled off a barrage of strange vernacular.

"Yes, Yes. You look like someone I know. Where you from? Barbados, Trinidad, Jamaica?" The man's small head matched his beady eyes. Paul attempted eye contact, but the man avoided it. Instead, he looked up at Paul's six foot four inch frame. Paul estimated him to be around five six or so as he took a step back. Paul didn't know if he was being sized up for an ensuing physical confrontation or what. "You look like someone I know from my Jamaica home," the man finally said.

"No Man. I am from the States, you know 'Frisco, San Francisco. I was wondering?" Paul tried to continue speaking but again he was cut off. The man's initial open and friendly demeanor seemed to change after discovering Paul was not from one of the places he'd mentioned.

"Yes, yes, well that's Cool, Brother. Look, you'll have to excuse me. I'm late for some very impo'tant business and here is my bus. If you're here t'morrow, maybe I can help you. You look like a good Brother. Later. Denny Phillips is my name."

The Brother did not wait for Paul to give him his name in return.

"Yeah, Yeah. Okay. Later, Man."

'Wow,' Paul thought to himself, 'that dude was talking so fast I don't even know what the fuck he said. Something about being here? Tomorrow?'

He searched for another congenial face. Eventually spotting someone, he thought, 'Now, that's a Cat that looks like he's from down home.'

Paul strode over to the approaching figure. Wearing a full-length leather coat with corduroy pinstriped bellbottoms, the man was looking very much like Richie Havens. A wild head of hair shaped in a huge afro and an overall mellow-looking demeanor completed his look.

"Say, Blood. I sure am glad to see you. Hey Dude, turn me on to the haps around here," said Paul. In the two days since he had arrived in Vancouver, this guy definitely looked like someone he could hang out with and talk out what this place was all about.

The Soul Brother was shaded down. Standing now directly in front of him, Paul could tell the man was high as a kite. His eyes were visible through the brown lenses of his glasses, but there was obviously no one home. Smoke, heroin, hashish? Made no difference. It was like back in Vietnam where every other soldier had been on one thing or another. In spite of this, Paul felt the Brother was someone he could relate to and so he continued his rap.

"Wow, a Homeboy," the man struggled to get out. "Yeah, Yeah. What it is, everything is everything, eh, eh, eh." He then stopped, as if he had forgotten what he just said, then repeated, "Wow, a Homeboy." He stopped conversing altogether and began looking up at the sky, frustrating Paul.

Paul spoke again, "Say Brother, do you read me or am I just talking to myself? You see, Blood, I just got back from 'Nam, you know, Vietnam, see, and I was wonderin' if..."

The Soul Brother interrupted. "Hey, Home. Good to see you, my Man. Turn me on to the haps, my Man." He then smiled widely, showing a row of teeth as yellow as a cob of corn that was missing several kernels. "Eh, eh, eh, you know Man, everything is everything."

Paul contained his frustration. He was more amused than curious about the Brother's state of consciousness as he gently lifted his own shades. No, definitely not Richie Havens here.

"Look, Dude. You're feeling pretty mellow right now...hey Blood?" This was an all too common encounter Paul had experienced many times with soldiers escaping their reality, completely loaded and simply not capable of pursuing any intelligible communication.

"Everything is everything, but time will take you on! That's James Brown talk. You do dig my man, James Brown?" the man actually waited for a definitive response.

Paul scratched his head and walked toward his hotel, leaving the Brother still talking, this time with his hands moving and drawing words in the air.

Paul had chosen to stay on at the Ritz, primarily because of its central downtown location. The lobby was alive and at the same time had a sense of organization. Everything had purpose and elegance from the furniture, to the bellmen, to the front desk.

Paul made his way to the Newsstand. "Can I buy a pack of Luckies?" he asked the Canadian salesgirl.

"No, Sir. But we have Marlboros or Salems."

"Marlboros then" Paul said. He decided to have some fun with the Canadian lady. "Why are all your bills different colors? People like to play Monopoly around here or something?"

She threw him a half-smile, sort of a come-on, while trying to maintain a very professional straight-laced demeanor. She was a statuesque brunette.

With a serious look on her face she said, "You Yanks are all alike. You come around here criticizing our money, criticizing our way of talking. Is that all they teach you Yankees down South? How to criticize? You won't make any friends through criticism, Sir. Try being a little more hospitable in your tone and you will receive it back."

"Down South Yankee! I have been called many a name, but Yankee? Damn," he said to the salesgirl. "Look, I'm sorry if I was giving you a hard time. I just got up here, you see, and I don't know what's going on and I have been desperately trying to find someone, anyone, who can just tell me where to go while I'm visiting Vancouver."

"Ah," the woman held up a finger and smiled. "If you are looking for places to go, there is always Pharaohs Retreat in Gastown, but that's a nightclub. Or you can try one of the pubs. Just across from this hotel, a few blocks away, is the Blue Horizon. Oh, and there's Oil Can Harry's just down the street."

"Hold it, hold it. Slow down, please. As I said, I just got here a couple of days ago. I've never been up here before. So why don't you break it down for me, you know, like nice and easy?"

"Well, tonight is a Friday night and our pub here at the Ritz is a great spot to enjoy the local scene. Yes, around about now the pub is starting to see people finishing their work day. I'm not into drinking beer myself, but it is a very popular pastime here in Canada."

Paul hesitated and then asked, "And what, pray tell, is a pub, dear lady?"

"What is a pub?" she repeated with astonishment in her voice. "A pub is where people go to drink beer and talk."

"Oh, you mean like a bar?"

"Yes, but much bigger and more lights. Best to go early, then you won't have to wait in line."

"Oh, is there some kind of cover charge to get into the pub?"

"Oh no, it's not that. It's just that the pub gets rather crowded on Fridays. People celebrating the start of their weekend."

"Thank you. I just might check it out."

The woman was maybe 20 or so, maybe mid-20s. Paul was never comfortable guessing people's ages. Nice shape though. Paul loved the way her greenish blue eyes seemed to change and sparkle during their conversation.

"Yes, you do that, Sir. I hope you enjoy your stay."

Her eyes lingered on Paul as he pivoted quickly and then turned back to her. He seemed to be a lot more articulate than most men of color she encountered in the hotel lobby.

She prided herself in being analytical. Sometimes it was her greatest asset but it could also be her greatest fault, depending on the circumstances.

She was currently in a relationship with a Black man and was constantly disappointed by the number of so-called 'cool people' who shot her disapproving looks behind his back. She had not chosen Enrico because he was Black. As a matter of fact, she often forgot he was Black. His way of talking, his mannerisms, and his 2000-watt gorgeous smile had swept her off her feet. When she'd met Enrico, she had been seduced by his *talk*, by his intellect and how he used it. She couldn't get enough of him. He told her stories, rich in detail, of all the places he'd been in the world. He explained politics and philosophies to her. Answering her many questions with respect and patience was never a problem. For him she was the perfect student, and he in turn made her feel alive and growing.

Now he was leaving town shortly. Off to another adventure. He had warned her, after only a week or so into their relationship that he was not here to stay. He was a hit n' run kinda guy. Wow them off their feet and exit while the audience is still clapping. Maybe his biggest fear was that the applause would come to an end. Enrico's ego was much too enormous to wait around for that to happen! She smiled to herself. He had made it clear that no one woman would be enough for him, but she saw through that weak bullshit. He could be *had* just like every other man she had conquered.

Her thoughts returned to Paul. Well, maybe she'd give this guy a twirl around the ol' dance floor. She could tell he was smart and kept his business close to his chest. Something about him reminded her of her own self. But she also knew that with her arsenal of physical attributes and worldly possessions, she could have any guy. Her question was always the same though: 'Were they worth the effort?' But this guy also had a megawatt smile and great looks. He was casual with an athletic build, unlike Enrico who was slender and very fastidious. Also, unlike Enrico, there was no arrogance. She made up her mind that she would see him again.

"Yes, thanks." Paul wanted to find out more about her, but thought it best to contain himself. He felt he was coming on too strong or...was he not being strong enough?

She sensed he was just standing there at a loss for words, so she said, "A handsome man like you will have no problem meeting new friends here in Vancouver. We're a hospitable lot."

'Whoa,' Paul thought to himself, 'these Canadians really are different.' Being from San Francisco, White, Black, Asian, Latino, whichever the nationality of the woman, they belonged to the cool gray city of love, San Francisco. All his buddies cried the same song and dance when it came to Bay Area women. Women always seemed to want to be courted and wooed to the tenth degree before you really knew where they were coming from.

Of course, he'd been forever involved with only one woman, JoAnn, and she had broken it down as showing proper etiquette. But Paul had been picking up a lot of good vibes from the ladies he was passing around this town. Proper etiquette meant saying what was on your mind, not trying to guess where the conversation was headed.

He thought, 'The two Brothers I spoke to earlier were cartoons, Looney Tune caricatures. I was almost ready to leave this town. But now, I think it may be worth staying for a while.'

A man with a strong Irish accent came up behind him and lightly tapped his shoulder. Paul was familiar with Irish accents from his early years of Catholic School at St. Michaels' and the many Daughters of Mary and Joseph nuns, directly off the boat from Ireland, who taught there. The man was rapidly growing impatient and Paul wanted to go on ignoring him - just because. But the Irishman was becoming so aggravated that the saleswoman paused in her conversation with Paul to ask the gentleman what he would like. The man requested a pack of Players cigarettes, paid, and abruptly brushed past Paul as he left.

As the guy walked away, Paul stood there thinking for a minute. 'That guy shouldn't have touched me whatsoever, but I'm willing to give him the benefit of doubt that he was not doing it out of disrespect. Whoever was in his path was simply in his way.'

The salesgirl sensed Paul had not liked the man physically brushing past him and spoke quickly to defuse the situation. "My name's Jennifer, Jennifer McAuley. Don't mind him. I went to a Catholic boarding school, most of the Irish priests and nuns were pushy like him. He meant no harm."

Paul exhaled and locked eyes with her once again. He wasn't a violent man, but he didn't like bullies. Anyway, he'd already come to the same conclusion.

She continued, "Enjoy the pub. Hopefully we'll be talking again."

"My name is Paul, by the way." He knew he would see her again. He thought about sharing with her his nine years of Catholic school education, something they seemingly had in common. But he decided that could be the focus of their next encounter or at least an opening rap.

As Jennifer watched Paul walk away, she decided it was time for a coffee break. That's what you do when your parents own the hotel - make your own break times. Enrico was the first man in her life for whom her family's money did not define her as a person, even though she loved the benefits that came with its reality. Enrico was accustomed to living with the rich and famous. He had actually helped her appreciate it for what it was: a hall pass through life, freedom to do whatever you damn well pleased, with discretion. 'And the people who know my past history would be overjoyed that Enrico was polishing the discretion part,' she laughed to herself.

She went across the lobby and settled in her favorite corner of the coffee shop. She took out a cigarette, lit it, and exhaled her first drag of the day, once again promising herself to stop smoking tomorrow. Someone had left a magazine next to her table with John Coltrane's picture on the cover. She recalled the first time she had been introduced to the likes of Coltrane, Miles Davis, and the world of smooth jazz. Not the crazy, incomprehensible, wild angry stuff. But the dreamlike, mystical ensembles and poetic voyages of the Master, John Coltrane. Music not for the lonely but for those who comfortably enjoyed being alone.

Her mind wandered back to the incident with the Irishman at the Newsstand and that reminded her of her school days. She remembered that day in Mother Superior's office with her parents. The Mother's soft, smug voice as she described the chaperons pushing through the cheering students to find Jennifer giving a blowjob to the student council president at the annual Richmond College-Little Rose Academy spring dance. As she listened to the details, she'd screamed in her head, NOW see ME, hear ME! Finally *SEE ME HEAR ME.*

But No, her parents' faces looked as if they would break as they closed off and shut her out. She knew the drill. Now they'd throw some big money at *this* problem to keep her in school 'til graduation.

At that moment, she had given up. 'No more. Color them gone from my life.' she had thought. They didn't care so she wouldn't care.

For the next year and a half, she'd been on a kind of lockdown. Driven to school, picked up afterwards, and taken directly to whichever psychiatrist she had an appointment with that day. The plan was to shrink her into submission. She played along. It wasn't hard *if you didn't care.* On the weekends, if her parents were away, she had 'a keeper.' If they were home, there were always guests and she played the perfect daughter. Polite answers, sweet demeanor, non-controversial clothes.

She honed what would become her most powerful survival skill, *being cool.* Don't say much, look aloof, show no emotion. She decided *Cool* was a necessary tool for navigating the world.

She was truly and completely alone. Her best friend since she was six years old had sunk into drug oblivion when they were in junior high. They used to tell their hearts to each other. It had always been Lidia and Jen. Oh God, how she missed her.

After graduation, her 'sentence served,' her parents agreed to the terms of her moving out to live on her own. To herself only, she had to admit she'd enjoyed decorating the apartment with her mom, except for the incident when she'd dipped the teacup she was holding into the painter's open can and poured the paint onto the huge mask they'd just hung. Her

Mom definitely did not embrace spontaneity, but in the end, they had both liked the result.

CHAPTER 8

THAT EVENING AT THE RITZ PUB, PAUL SPENT HALF an hour observing the sea of gray faces from one corner to another. White Folks. 'But it's really strange,' he thought to himself, 'I have received lots of looks over this way, but they ain't the same as the looks from White folks in the States. Longhairs, business types, men and ladies of all ages, giving questioning looks, like wondering if I'm some sort of celebrity - maybe Sidney Poitier,' he thought in jest. Maybe these people *are* different. Back in 'Nam, most places were segregated. The Whites had their bars and the Brothers had theirs. And having been raised in California, that experience had been something totally new to him.

A man with a Fu Manchu mustache approached Paul and introduced himself. He was wearing a Western-style outfit - hat, coat, boots, long hair...the works. He even looked a little like Wild Bill Hickok. "Say, Brother. Just pass this by if I'm wrong, but didn't you play bass guitar for a while back in San Francisco?"

Paul looked up, at first trying to maintain an indifferent look, then vaguely placing the guy's face somewhere in his head. The Canadian beer was stronger than expected and he had to pee again. "Yeah, Man. But that was a long time ago."

"Right on! Lowell High, right? Too Much, Man! Your group edged our group out by two votes in one of the school talent shows. Remember?"

"Yeah, sort of, but if I'm not mistaken, didn't your group come back the next month and beat us by five votes?"

"Far Fucking Out! Yeah, Man, that's it. Say, look, my name is Steve Hasen and yours is Paul. Paul Marshall, right?"

Paul nodded his head. "Yeah, that's me." He was pleasantly surprised and happy to finally be talking to someone from home. Paul recalled this guy sitting across from his desk in the same homeroom back at school. And Wow, he had actually remembered his name.

"I always wanted to shake your hand, Man. All them sports you played and mastering a pick as well. Far Fucking Out! Say, we were in the same homeroom. I was a lot smaller then. Oh, and no mustache, of course. How long are you going to be here?"

He extended his hand, and they shook hands firmly.

"You know, Man, I don't know," Paul said. "I just came up, you know, to check the place out. Just finished a tour in 'Nam and decided I wasn't ready to stay in San Francisco."

"Say look," Steve replied, "why don't you come on over to our table and meet some friends of mine?" Paul couldn't see why not. He got up and followed Steve to a far corner table. "Paul, this is Bill Marcos from Toronto, our lead guitarist; and Sammy Stevens from Seattle, our drummer. Guys, this is Paul Marshall, a friend from San Francisco. We were in high school together."

Bill stood up to shake his hand. Sammy kept on drinking.

"So you two Yankees graduated from the same school?" Bill asked in a surprised voice.

'Damn, I'm being called a Yankee again!' Paul thought to himself.

"Yeah," said Steve, "but Paul went off to Vietnam. You were in the ROTC, weren't you?"

Before Paul could answer that he wasn't, Sammy all of a sudden seemed to sober up. He blurted out, "Say, is this the new bass guitarist you promised us?" Sammy's tone was aggressive and loud.

"Say what?" said Paul.

"Wait a minute," said Steve. "Fellows, the Man plays a mean bass pick, but our man is coming at ten o'clock. Remember?"

"Say Man, what's this all about?" asked Paul.

"Well, we are supposed to start a two-week gig at Oil Cans down the street next Wednesday, and our bass pick man copped out on us."

"You mean the dude just split?" said Paul.

A blasted Sammy jumped up and planted himself directly in front of Paul. "No Man, he croaked. You know, Man. D-E-A-D!"

"Cool it," said Steve. "Cool it, Sammy. It wasn't anybody's fault but his." Trying to calm Sammy down, Steve got up and positioned himself between the two men.

"Bullshit!" Sammy continued yelling and showering everyone in close range with spit. "You know who killed him? They did!" he cried, as he pointed out at the crowd. Angry, hostile emotions seem to fall out of his mouth like a full meal parting from his gut. "This fucking plastic spaceship, liars, cheats, cockhounds. Man, you dudes think you got so much trouble being Black and shit. Everybody on your back. Well, your people ain't the only ones who have to eat those capitalist bastards' bullshit. Man, our manager didn't even give a damn about Mark when he croaked. The only thing the bastard wanted to know was if we could replace him before our opening."

The guy appeared ready to rant the whole rest of the night, but Steve cut him off.

"Cool it. Cool it, Sammy," said Steve. "You are walking on thin ice, Man. Ain't Paul's problem. Cool it!"

Sammy went back over to his seat, chugged his beer, and stomped out of the pub.

Paul stood there not even attempting to take a seat as Sammy stormed passed him, moving straight for the door.

"Look, Man. Nice meeting you. I'd better go after Sammy," said Bill, who up to that moment had appeared slightly disinterested in the goings on.

Steve gestured for Paul to take a seat as he reclaimed his chair. "Ignore Sammy. He really is a good man; he's just been pretty uptight lately. Plus, he overmedicates a lot, trying to freeze those brain cells. And I'm not talking about prescription drugs, Dig? It's a pity he has to fly off to the dark side before he can let go of what he's feeling." He continued, "Oh, and be prepared for folks up here to come at you direct as Sammy. You know, comparing his woes to the Negro plight." Steve put extra emphasis on *Negro*.

Paul smiled back. "Canadians do know we colored folks prefer the term 'Afro-American' these days or Black even...but NEGRO is passé," Paul explained, trying to bring some levity to the conversation.

Steve laughed back. "I think he's Canadian? But, barely! Shit, the *Negro Problem* up here doesn't even involve Afro-Americans. The colored folks up here are the Native-Americans, the Indians. I had a lady I was dating and she was an Indian or First Nation, whatever." Steve seemed to get his hands moving about the air with each syllable from his mouth. "She had me meet her one night at a NAACP meeting!"

Paul gulped down his beer and leaned in closer to Steve. "Did she have *Brothers* in her family?"

"Hell, Dude," Steve replied. "The Red Man is the downtrodden in this part of Canada. They're the ones in the government-assisted housing. Yeah, they have Projects up here too and it's primarily Native Indians living there. It's a trip."

"Yeah," Paul retorted. "Guess everybody's got to have their Niggers?"

"Yeah," Steve replied "I hear in Asian countries it's the Koreans, and in Russia it's the Ukrainians. Great Britain, the Irish. Eastern Canada, the French Canadians."

Paul nodded his head, and Steve said, "Well, I'm sorry you didn't get to meet the boys."

"That's Cool, man. I expect that kind of shit every now and then. The Dude's obviously upset. Were they close friends?" said Paul.

"We've been playing as a group now for a couple of years. So yeah, we were all tight, but shit happens. Well look, Man. How long you planning on being in Vancouver?" asked Steve.

"Just for awhile. I haven't decided yet, but you know."

"Yeah. Listen it's 6:30 now. Look, if you want to check out Oil Cans later, ask for the big black-haired dude with the Fu Manchu mustache like mine. Name's Tom. Tell him you're a friend of mine and he'll let you in free, compliments of the house, and I'll try to get by your hotel before you split... Here right?"

"Yeah I'm staying here. Thanks Man. I just might check the place out. Later!" said Paul and he left.

CHAPTER 9

AS PAUL WALKED OUT OF THE PUB, HE NOTICED THE salesgirl, Jennifer, waiting on the sidewalk in front of the hotel. He walked over to her.

"Well, how you doing? Thanks for the hook up. The pub was a blast!"

"Oh, it's you. How are you? Enjoyed the pub?" she replied, as if they had known each other for years.

As Paul eyed the girl up and down, he said to himself, 'She must want something to be so friendly.'

She didn't let him respond before she added, "Did I tell you?.. you remind me of someone. His name is Enrico. He's my lover." Before Paul could reply she waved, "Enrico! Enrico! Over here." And 'Enrico' pulled over in a shiny Austin-Healey. An attractive, dark, deep mahogany-complexioned man got out and walked over to them. Paul laughed to himself. 'Ain't no way this guy's from The States. He's as dark complexioned as I am but he's wearing his raven black hair in a long thick braid.' His face was chiseled with a sharp nose and high cheekbones. Paul figured that Enrico must be South American Indian or something.

"Enrico, I want you to meet...what did you say your name was again?" she asked.

Paul felt dejected. Jennifer had been so open and warm a moment ago and now she didn't even remember his name. Then he caught on - she was putting on a show for her lover man. Paul waved both hands in the air laughing to himself, "Look, I gotta go."

Enrico interjected abruptly: "No. No, wait a minute. I heard about you. How are you, my Brother? What's happening? Como Esta?"

Paul looked over at the man. "Yeah. What's happening?" He seemed like a pretty cool dude. But he still couldn't place where he was from. He was Black, but not from any of the obvious countries.

"You're not from here. How long are you going to be here? Have you seen much of the city?" Enrico asked Paul.

"No, I haven't."

"Well then, Amigo. Why don't you let us take you home? Treat you to some dinner, drinks or something, and maybe we can show you around?" The man was so sincere and gracious.

Paul quickly put up his guard. This couldn't be real. "No. No, that's okay." he weakly replied.

"Come," beckoned Jennifer in a sexy tone. "Come on! It'll be fun! I told Enrico about you earlier," she murmured as she linked her arm with Paul. "Of course I remembered your name. I was just playing with you. Enrico blew my cover. I did tell him about our encounter. You know, with the Irish guy and such."

Paul looked at the man, looked at her, and said, "Why not?"

Enrico was driving the slick little sports car, top down. Instead of Jennifer jumping in the back of this obvious two-seater, she told Paul to get in first and then sat on his lap. She smelled and felt heavenly.

Enrico and Jennifer were pointing out various points of interest in all directions. They only seemed to drive a short distance. Too bad, Paul was hoping she could sit there a whole lot longer. When the car stopped, they were in front of one of the tallest buildings on the block.

Jennifer stated with authority, "Remember this address. We are in the English Bay section of the West End and our apartment complex is the Beach Towers. There are actually three towers and ours is the one closest to the beach directly across the street. Most people know it. We have one of the best views in Vancouver."

Next to the apartments was yet another small park with an old Bandstand in the middle. Jennifer reminded Paul that it was almost Summer Solstice, the longest day of the year. That, along with Vancouver being as far north as it was, meant that dusk lasted long after the sun had set. In fact, it wouldn't be fully dark 'til around 10:30 at this time of year.

They took an elevator to the highest floor of the building. Inside the apartment, the place was outstanding: everything exuded money. Along one wall was a white lacquered, long low console with a sleek sound system sitting on one end. Facing the floor to ceiling wall of window was a curved, off-white couch sitting on a Flokati rug with an oversized chrome and glass coffee table in front of it. From the corner arced a huge silver globe that cast a soft glow on the table. That was the only light in the room. On the other wall hung a four-foot African mask carved out of wood that someone had poured white paint on.

The focal point of the apartment was the view, which explained the unusual placement of the couch. Jennifer told him they could see all the way to Vancouver Island. Paul looked out at the U-shaped bay with city lights sparkling on either side interspersed with patches of forest then an unobstructed view of the ocean with the faint outline of mountains in the very far distance. A number of freight ships speckled the bay, anchored, waiting their turn to dock.

Paul thought back to his Uncle Melvin's penthouse apartment on Nob Hill, the swankiest place he'd seen 'til now. He had finally found a rival for his uncle's sophisticated style. The views were similar, but Melvin's view faced north, across the bay with Alcatraz Island and Angel Island as the focal point.

This view looked west. The setting sun peeked just above a sheet of gray black solid layer cloud with a white rim that formed a sideways horseshoe shape in the very blue sky. Sunrays projected down into the open horseshoe space leaving a majestic white glow over the now darkened sea.

"So you call this Summer what?" asked Paul.

"Summer Solstice…almost. Nice sunset, don't you think?" Jennifer replied. She did not wait for a response, but just walked over to the stereo and broke out the smooth soft jazz of John Coltrane's "In a Sentimental Mood." Enrico wasted no time firing up a fat joint. Taking a toke of the fragrant, pungent smoke, he passed it over to Paul.

"I notice you haven't said anything about your departure?" Jennifer said to Enrico. She seemed to just pluck that out of the air from nowhere. "Aren't you going to tell Paul about your next great adventure?" Paul noticed her voice was *velvet affection with a hint of resentment.* Enrico shrugged his shoulders, not showing any significant reaction one way or the other.

Paul took another long drag on the joint and looked over at Jennifer. The entire apartment smelled like the rich perfume she was wearing. The aroma melded with the smoke and created a heady, sensual smell. But something here was not jiving. She worked at a job well below her sharp, witty, intelligence level and beauty. Was it the Brother's crib? Absolutely not, Paul concluded. With so much going for her, why was the dude Enrico leaving? Paul started laughing to himself. Whatever the reason was, it was Enrico's loss and *his* gain… maybe?

A heavy silence hung in the air. Paul sensed that bullets were about to fly between Jennifer and Enrico. He definitely was not here to play Dear Abby, so he decided to intervene, to divert the scene.

"This place ain't any different than any other place I've been to," he said, knowing he was purposefully starting something. "The people ain't shit. Vancouver ain't shit! I almost had to get physical with this dude in the pub who jumped in my face."

Enrico took the bait. "C'mon, man. You're still relating with your U.S. of A. labels. We're not like the ones you meet in that chaos down South. Though I'm not Canadian, I have travelled a sufficient number of places in the world to compare it to and I tell you that I absolutely love this place and its people. I have a Fifth Degree Black Belt, but I can't remember the last time I had to get physical with some chump. There's always another way to control the situation. Besides, this sounds cliché, but violence does escalate shit."

"I don't know Man," Paul shot back, "lots of different kinds of people where I come from in San Francisco. Where I've just been, you know, 'Nam, you back down too many times and someone's gonna whip your ass! But I guess you believe in all this Love Generation shit, ah? Is that what it is, Enrico?"

"Hey take it easy," Enrico said. "Hombre, Mi Amigo. You're only listening halfway. I ain't afraid of getting down, when necessary. I'm just saying there's usually another way of dealing with most situations."

As he got up from his chair he beckoned Paul to come and enjoy the view from the balcony overlooking English Bay. Jennifer was standing there with a glass of wine looking out at the sea.

"I'm just curious. How old are you?"

Paul answered, "Twenty-one, why?"

"Well, let's see. I think I was like you when I was that age. Yes, just like you. Bitter at the world, angry, and not knowing why I felt that way. But I've seen a bit now. I've seen a bit more. I've met more people and been to more places. I've traveled the world, met a lot more faces. I'm thirty now, Man."

"Well, Congratulations. Thirty years old," Paul said very sarcastically.

"Yes, yes. Thirty. I've travelled most of the world. Come a long way from the slums of Panama, and I've managed to travel first class as well as hop freighters. Man, I will say this for Vancouver, there are more people willing to unveil their masks here than any other place I've been to."

"Man," said Paul, "I really can't disagree or agree with you at this point. All I can say is I've been here..." he made a show of checking his watch, "that many hours, but this place don't seem no different from the States. Same Shell Stations, same McDonald's, same Marlboros, same Fords, everything. Just an hour ago, I almost had to physically subdue one of my boys for trying to loud-talk me." He caught himself repeating what he'd said earlier...must be the smoke.

"Yes, yes, my Brother, the devil is all over. What I'm trying to say is this - I've worked out this little theory, taken me a while. I guess it's been cooking in my head since I was about thirteen, but anyway I worked out this theory that says there is a significance to the watch on your wrist. The face of the watch is just another type of face, another mask to be used as required, like 'Oh My, look at the time, gotta go.'

"There are an array of masks to choose from. A mask for fear, a mask for prejudice, a mask for happiness, a mask for success, a mask for pleasure. One face with all these different masks stacked one on top of the other. We've developed ways to use them at work, outside of work, at parties...for all occasions. And it turns out that all over the world, people with their masks are being controlled by something that is simply ticking away. Time passing, passing time with the least amount of mental engagement. A lazy way to not engage. Not be present.

"But at some point, a conflict arises of whether you are controlling the masks or they are controlling you. One forgets that the stupid mask is outwardly showing where you in the present interaction. And somehow, no one is supposed to comment on a mask of indifference or other times straight up rudeness to the person directly in front of you. Why let a phony mask run your life? If you're interested in the person in front of you or not, let them know. Live in the moment, engage, and let them know what you are feeling regarding their conversation."

"Well," Paul said, "I stand accused, Hombre. I just tune them out. Drift off to another space in time."

"You must always be in control of every emotion you choose to portray at every moment in time. There should never be a time when you have not already anticipated the next move of whatever game you have fallen into playing or when you have had enough of the person in front of you. When somebody reveals a certain emotion and you know they're moving towards your panic button, either you move another way or you accept and confront. Maybe even try to understand why the situation is causing you to consider pushing a panic button. Maybe even learn something about yourself that may save your life one day. Never be afraid of learning more, especially about yourself. See where I'm coming from?" he asked.

"I mean, what happens when our masks fall away; do we see the real person?" Paul quietly asked, "or do *their* masks block getting any meaningful interaction back?"

"Most people can't deal with the naked truth. Most people are in some sort of transition. In fact, the best of us are always in some stage of transition. They may not even know where they are going with the conversation. But it doesn't hurt for you to listen, and if you realize at some point the person is chattering gibberish, then allow them the level of respect you feel they deserve...be it changing the conversation or calling their attention to what's coming out of their mouths. You may not be the most popular guy in their lives, but again you may gain more from the interaction than you would have otherwise.

"You see, I enjoy identifying the individual's mask and watching them get so much more at ease with me by giving them an excuse or reason to let down their guard or drop that mask and be open to whatever may come next." Enrico's face broke into a big grin that seemed to light up the space. Was he was really breathing his own fumes and enjoying listening to himself? Or was *he* just talking gibberish?

"So you never abuse or make the person sorry for trusting you?" Paul countered.

"Amigo, you are making things far too complicated. I'm just getting them to enjoy *now*. Enjoy the present moment and place we are in. They don't have to agree to anything. I'm not professing a Nietzsche type headset, you know 'whatever does not kill you, makes you stronger' or 'pain must come before one can truly enjoy pleasure.' *Simply own what you are selling.* My time is important to me and I trust they feel the same. But if that is not their belief at that moment in time, then that's their choice. This is how I live my life. Baby, I'm for real. And to 90 percent of them, I represent progress," he laughed, "not more bull crap."

"And what happens to the other 10 percenters?" asked Paul.

"For them, life simply remains the same. All I'm hoping for is to plant the seed of change. I cannot guarantee the sunshine or water necessary for growth.

"I think it was the Englishman, T. S. Eliot, who once said, 'Between the conception and the creation Between the emotion and the response Falls the Shadow.' Life is very long and what makes it even longer or more difficult is not adjusting to the masks - masks you created and masks you should master, not the other way around. We all share common fears, common hopes, and common pleasures."

Paul felt himself becoming mesmerized by the way Enrico was talking with his hands. The man had lost him a few sentences back. Growing up in the City, lots of folks had talked with their hands, especially the Italians. He knew Steve was Jewish and Enrico was from Panama so obviously neither were Italian. Paul laughed to himself, 'but they sure talk with their hands like they are.'

Enrico could not ignore Paul's perplexed stare. Was it from an attempt to really understand him or was he simply in a mind freeze from the smoke and wine? He looked like a bright kid and there was something about Paul that made you want to impress him.

"Yes, My Brother. I feel like you know what I'm attempting to explain, what I'm trying to say. Now enough of me. Let me speak directly to you. You got to open up and stop trying to second-guess the man. If a gift is handed to you, don't overanalyze it. Accept whatever. Frequently the situation coming in your direction really has nothing to do with you as a person. It is only an opportunity to act out some shit that someone else is experiencing and feels the need to express. I get the feeling you may have some issues regarding a past relationship. Hell. I don't know anything about you, but I'm vibing this is the case. But Amigo, dig this: love can turn sour and you may have been the cause. But even Enrico knows he cannot control everything, and *that* my friend is the Challenge and Beauty of Life."

Paul got up and stretched. "Yeah Man, I get what you're saying, I think. But it's been a very long day. I gotta get some sleep. I have a decision to make tomorrow. Should I stay or should I go?"

His last statement required no response. Enrico was cool with that. He reached into his pocket, lit a cigarette, and without any more words started walking with him towards the front door.

Jennifer had disappeared a while ago. Paul noticed the bedroom door was ajar as they passed and he glanced in. She was laying on her side, looking at television, her back to the door. She wore sheer panties, outlining some of the finest thighs and ass he had ever seen, like something out of a *Playboy Magazine*.

Enrico offered to drive him back to his hotel. As they stepped into the elevator, he suggested a nightcap at a place en route to the hotel. Paul accepted. They drove a couple of blocks and parked in front of a shiny black door with the address in small raised silver numbers. There was no sign and no handle on the door but Enrico pressed a button concealed on the side and only a minute later, the door swung open. Inside Paul could see this small club was built out over the ocean. The walls were lined with wood and the carpet was dark and plush in the subdued lighting. Enrico was greeted as if he were royalty by the host. The hot waitresses wore short black dresses with tall platform shoes showing lots of leg in fishnet stockings.

"Damn, Bro. This place is rather impressive," said Paul.

"Yes, we come here often. All the major movers in this town are seen here."

Paul couldn't wait any longer to ask. "Enrico, what do you do for a living?"

"I'm an entertainer of sorts. I entertain women's hearts," Enrico calmly replied. "Some people use the word gigolo. Whatever the title, ladies pay me to look good. To make them look good. And I do what I do well. Some may want to define me as a shylock, a merciless *user* created by Shakespeare. Many times I wish I could be without a heart. But the honest truth is I love women. Everything there is about women. Their walk, their style, their hormonal shifts, and their visions of life."

"Visions of life?" Paul asked incredulously.

"Si Amigo. It's not just about the hormones. The world focuses on who was allegedly created in God's very image, *Man*. Women have an advantage. They know who they have to get over to be successful in life: whichever male is *in charge*, that's the target. Many times the male ego will not even see a woman as a serious competitor, because the male is focusing on another male competing for his spot, his domain. I love to educate the so-called 'weaker sex' as to how powerful they really are.

"Mary Magdalene was the wife of Jesus Christ. She sits next to her husband in the painting, *The Last Supper* by Leonardo da Vinci. The Bible says she was a reformed prostitute and was with Christ at the crucifixion and the resurrection. But if you look at the work of da Vinci, she is there at *The Last Supper*. Therefore, she was in Christ's life before the crucifixion. *Power*, Amigo. The Catholic Church will never truly recognize a woman could be just as competent a priest as a man, because they are fearful of the woman's potential for total power, and yes Amigo, *control*."

"Damn!" responded Paul, "that is brilliant." He was truly impressed. The dude was definitely long-winded but a lot of his shit made sense. What Paul still couldn't figure out is why Enrico would walk away from a setup like he had with Jennifer. Paul again flashed on the image of Jennifer in the bedroom as they were leaving. "But your lady, Jennifer, she works at the hotel, selling cigarettes and newspapers. How does she support your lifestyle?" Paul asked.

"Jennifer's family has lots of money," Enrico replied. "Her parents have only one stipulation: she has to work to continue their support. That woman has one weakness - me. But then again, they all do sooner or later. I am Magnificent." Enrico then stood up to model his leather bell bottoms and silk shirt that matched his shiny maroon Austin-Healey. "*Stunning*, to sum it up in a word.

"My problem is I bore easily. I never take all their money. I will stay for a while and then I'm off again. In fact, Jennifer was alluding to that tonight. I've been asked to join another lady friend in New York. Have you been there? Love New York. Then we're off to her villa in Italy. You see, my friend, the sooner you realize your true talent life can become so much more interesting. Whatever your true talent may be."

Paul sensed the brother was not looking to debate the issue nor was he interested in Paul's personal opinions. But

Paul was not satisfied with what was being offered. He fell into the next obvious question: "And what is your talent?"

Enrico took out a coin from his pocket, a dime from the United States of America. He then took a glass of water and sipped it a little. It appeared that he was trying to get the perfect level of liquid in the glass. And then he positioned the glass at an angle, placing a bottom edge of the glass onto the coin between the head of President Roosevelt and the outer rim. It worked. The glass sat balanced at a 45-degree angle on the head of the dime.

Paul tried not to look impressed. Before he could say anything, Enrico held up a finger to silence him.

"*Control*, my friend; I am sharing with you a lesson in control. This little trick used at the right time, the correct moment in the conversation, has placed me exactly where I'd planned to be more times than you can ever imagine." Moving the conversation away from himself, Enrico said, "Jennifer likes you. You have an opportunity awaiting you when I leave. You may find many women here in Vancouver, but none that will take care of you the way I have taught her to treat a man. Maybe we will meet again someday, you and me. But that is not important. If you're still in her life when I choose to return, I will have her back. I am certain of this. So I am sharing.

"You may say it's her choice, not mine, who she chooses to be with. Well, my friend. I don't look at it that way. When I am granted access into their minds, I possess them forever. No man is considered a threat to me, because I am in control until I choose to release that control." He paused to sip his drink.

"Are you listening to me, Amigo? It only takes me a few minutes to know who else in the room may possess my gift. And you are blessed with this gift as well. The *gift of control*. It is God-given. It cannot be learned, manufactured or purchased. Think how you will choose to use it. This is how I have chosen to use it." He spread his arms in a grandiose gesture. Enrico then abruptly stopped his speech, stood up, and said, "You must excuse me, my friend. I see someone over in the corner I must speak with tonight."

He then lifted the glass of water off the dime, set it back on the table, and left.

Paul felt this was the perfect time to get back to the hotel, so he asked a waitress for directions and split.

CHAPTER 10

WAKING UP EARLY THE FOLLOWING MORNING, PAUL decided to have breakfast and look around the town. Enrico's words vibrated in his head. He held the power to make his next move in taking control of his life. As the elevator door opened to the lobby, he heard a lively and loud conversation going on in the adjacent corner. As he drew closer, he noticed that the man engaged in the conversation was none other than Steve Hasen.

It sounded like Steve had just been seriously busted with another woman. The conversation was truly live. A beautiful redhead was demanding an explanation as to why he was in the hotel lobby when he'd told her he was taking care of a sick friend. Apparently, someone had told her Steve was there with another friend of hers. Now Steve's hands were waving every which way as she stood toe-to-toe and face-to-face with him. And she wasn't buying any of it.

Paul had decided to ignore it all and walk past the two when Steve came running over to him.

"Paul. Paul, I'm glad you down, Man. You ready to go?"

The woman followed him, exposing a blue satin nightgown covered by a full-length fur coat. It was obvious she had come to the hotel in a hurry. Her hair looked a mess, but overall, this woman was definitely hot.

"I'm tired of this shit. I can't take this much longer," he babbled on, while flapping his arms and hands like Elmer Gantry preaching a sermon. "Paul, I want you to meet somebody, even though she ain't worth being introduced to," rolling his eyes like Eddie Cantor doing black face.

This was a White Man working it. He was rapping like there was no tomorrow, seriously laying down his *talk*. He then abruptly stopped everything, the hand waving, the mouth running, and said to her, "Look Babe, I'm taking my man Paul out for some grub. You just believe whatever you want to believe and we will talk more about you sneaking around trying to catch me doing something that only exists in that pretty little head of yours." He then threw an arm over Paul's shoulders and they walked through the lobby and out of the hotel.

Paul had to give it to Steve; he was one cool dude. He stood about six feet even, which was impressive in itself, as Paul recalled he had been no more than five foot six back in high school when they'd played basketball together. Paul was a star for the Varsity team and Steve was Junior Varsity. Super quick with his hands and the ball, he'd scrimmaged more with the Varsity than the JV's. If the guards for the Varsity had not been state champion caliber, Steve likely would have made the Varsity squad.

His swift hands were obviously a talent that worked well for a lead guitarist too, as now he was the vocals and second lead guitarist for a group called Ecstasy.

Steve Hasen had gotten a real rep with the ladies. He had been the talk of their school and was even voted Best Looking Guy for their graduating class. He'd told Paul last night that between the first year and second year of attending San Francisco State, he'd made some awesome connections with people in the music industry. But then he'd pissed off the wrong 'Important People' and ended up leaving the city and coming to Canada.

His talent was phenomenal. This was what Enrico and Jennifer had told Paul last night when he'd mentioned who he'd been drinking with at the pub. With a voice range spanning Andy Gibb and Otis Redding, he could blend into any scene. He liked to identify himself as White Soul, with a little Joe Crocker or even Tom Jones mixed in.

Paul had looked forward to checking out the dude, but he hadn't expected to see him this morning.

Outside waiting in front of the hotel, was a beautiful silver Mercedes Coupe with California license plates. "Here we are." said Steve, "I'll introduce you to the town righteously. We're going to this cool place across the Lions Gate Bridge. They serve some really good breakfast there."

As he revved up the engine, Steve opened the glove compartment, pulled out a hashish pipe, and handed it to Paul. He started laughing, obviously very pleased with himself. Taking the pipe back, he used his lap and a Swiss Army knife to chop off a piece of rock, lit up, took a long drag on the pipe and then passed it back to Paul. Thinking back to Vietnam, Paul recalled the first time he'd ingested opium-laced hashish in the jungle with his troop. It was something he had done often when he was a Marine. The damnedest thing was how it had never impaired the job at hand, be it sewing up and bandaging a wound or setting a broken leg. All was good, as long as he stayed away from the hard stuff, heroin and acid trips, but maryj and hash were routine shit. The warning of *Try the Big H once and you're hooked for life* had stuck with Paul, so he'd never tried it. He liked to be in control too much to fight with a heroin monkey clinging to his back.

As he pulled out into traffic, Steve laid out what had just happened back at the hotel. "Did you see the look on her face, Man? Did you see where she was coming from? Total desperation or should I say failure in not accomplishing her mission, which was to finally bust my ass. Ain't that some shit." Steve went on, "Yeah Man, let me catch you up on what happened. You see last night...Oh by the way that dude never did show up, the bass guitarist. Anyway, last night after you left, I went over to Sherry's house, that's the redhead's name, Sherry. Anyway, she had this girlfriend visiting her from Alberta. Well, I could see right off that me and the Alberta chick had a few things in common, like both being sex freaks. Dig. I mean like the way her legs were gap toward me and what not. So she made up this thing about how she had to go because she was tired and had to get up early, just like I laid it out to her, planning to hook up with her where she was staying. See she's an airline stewardess for Air Canada and was just here overnight. Left this morning around five and I guess I fell back asleep.

"Anyway, I had actually fucked the shit out of Sherry before I told her one of my partners was ill and staying at my crib, so I had to get back. Usually we would be rocking on through the morning light. Oh but I do get greedy from time to time. I crept on over to this hotel which just happened to be the same one you were at. I kinda remembered you saying you were here. I'm always thinking about a backdoor escape. You know, like Mike Connors in *Tightrope*. Well, it sure came in handy today."

Steve laughed again, heading down the street away from the hotel. As they drove past, Paul recognized Denman St. where Enrico and Jennifer lived. Here the road curved and they were in a park, Stanley Park, Steve told him. It reminded Paul a lot of Golden Gate Park in San Francisco. On one side of the roadway was a small lake with a fountain in the middle, and on the other side, another road turned into the park just past what looked like a Yacht Club. They drove on a ways through a forest then across the Lions Gate Bridge.

The smoke had him drifting back to the smell of Jennifer's perfume and that body. It had been a long time since Paul had slept with JoAnn. When the other guys had taken to the brothels, Paul had abstained, saying to himself that it would be that much sweeter when he and his Girl were together again. Wow, was he wrong about that one!

"Now this has an uncanny resemblance to the Golden Gate Bridge, only shorter," said Paul.

"Hey Man! That's exactly what I said when I saw it the first time," Steve replied excitedly. "So I did a little research, and guess what? This one was totally inspired by the Golden Gate. It was privately built by some wealthy English family who were financing a residential suburb in West Vancouver they called 'British Properties'. The British Properties' chicks would be like the rich girls in Marin County or down the

South Bay in Hillsborough or even in the city over in the Presidio or Washington Heights districts. Where the young ladies' daddies are rich and their mommas are bored. Money and boredom make a dangerous combination. I try and exploit that disease when and wherever I can!" Steve exclaimed.

Over the bridge, they turned east to North Vancouver and Steve's destination. The Tomahawk. The restaurant had a huge totem pole in front of it, and the food was as good and plentiful as promised.

After breakfast, Steve decided to drive Paul up Grouse Mountain, stopping to walk across the Capilano Suspension Bridge. As they got out of the car, Paul noticed a casually dressed Brother with a cropped afro. They greeted each other as they passed. For whatever reason, Paul decided to check his back pocket for his wallet, thinking he may have left it on the car seat.

As he moved his hand, he made contact with the Brother's hand, apparently also going for Paul's back pocket. As their hands grazed, the man smoothly moved his away and apologized lightly for the subtle contact. Paul didn't know if it was an intentional move to pickpocket him or an innocent graze of hands. It did not warrant a confrontation, but it did heighten Paul's awareness. He was more disappointed than angry.

Steve had observed the interaction, laughed, and said, "Be careful. Not all who seem to be your Brother are really looking out for you."

Paul's reaction at that point was to confront the dude, but as he turned around, the man had literally blended into the passing crowd and disappeared. Lesson learned, and well stated by his new friend Steve.

"Let's roll on up to Grouse Mountain and sip on some brews or something," suggested Steve as he put his hand on Paul's shoulder and guided him back to the car.

To reach the restaurant at the top of the mountain, they had a seven or eight minute ride on a gondola. 'What a fantastic view!' Paul exclaimed to himself, not wanting to sound like a school kid on a field trip. At the top, they walked over to the restaurant called The Grouse Nest and took a table by the window where the view was even more spectacular. Stanley

Park dominated Paul's attention as they had just driven through it, but there was so much more to see. Straight in front of them, actually south facing, the Burrard Inlet gave Vancouver the appearance of being a peninsula like San Francisco. Beyond the Park was the bay Paul recognized from last night. Steve pointed out, as had Jennifer and Enrico, that the far side of the bay was the Kitsilano area of the city where the University of British Columbia sat at the farthest tip surrounded by ocean and what appeared from this distance to be another forest. Beyond that stretched a huge residential section with another body of water cutting through it.

"What's that?" asked Paul.

"Not really sure. But if you see the airport out there, it might be the Fraser River," said Steve. Can't see that far, if truth be told, but glasses would ruin my hip look, don't you think?"

Still looking south, a faint snow-covered peak stood alone. It was Mount Baker which he later learnt was actually across the border in the U.S.A. The commanding view before them was Vancouver and all its suburbs in one eyeful.

In the other direction further up the inlet was another more modern looking bridge. Paul figured they must be looking east. Along one side of the inlet close to this other bridge was a cluster of cylindrical structures with three freight ships docked in front of huge cranes. Being raised in the city, neither Steve nor Paul had a clue as to what their actual function was, but thought maybe they were used for storing something like wheat or other grain. Beyond the bridge on the other side from where they were was a series of hills. At the top of the furthest one, above the trees, was a cluster of concrete buildings that caught Paul's attention. They were only slightly visible and again Steve had no idea of what they were. It was obvious his buddy Steve's focus was the downtown area of Vancouver.

Both men seemed to be caught up in their own heads. Paul's mind was still boggled with all the words hammered down by Enrico. 'And the man was just handing over his woman, as if throwing the car keys to me.' Paul thought to himself. Could it be that simple?

Steve had stopped rapping for the first time since leaving the hotel. It seemed he was thinking back to this morning... maybe? Paul studied the look on his face. He could not remember a time in his life when two people so caught up in an argument could simply walk away from each other without some type of physical contact, like a slap in the face or a good shaking..something. What did that say about this guy? 'Well,' thought Paul, 'time will reveal what this Dude's about.'

He again turned to the amazing view outside and resumed his thoughts.

He had left Stanford during his second year. Maybe he should consider going back to college. After all, he'd heard Enrico loud and clear. He had the power to do whatever he chose to do. He had stood up to his parents regarding his decision on not going to law school. JoAnn's departure from his life hurt, but he had to admit he was to blame. It was a wrong choice on his part not to stay in contact with her or at least clue her in on his move to join the Marines and end up in Vietnam.

Paul later found out that the cement structures sitting on the mountaintop was the other major university in the area called Simon Fraser. Something seemed to be calling to him from that place atop Burnaby Mountain, as Steve called it.

How ironic he had found himself thinking about living in another city built on a peninsula. Actually, although there was lots of ocean in and around Vancouver, it could not be defined a peninsula - surrounded by water on three sides and connected to the mainland, as Paul had first thought. Steve had broken down Vancouver's geography to him, as only a fellow San Franciscan could break it down. There was no Oakland Bay Bridge to the east or Golden Gate Bridge to the north, as existed in their city.

Well, he had enough cash saved to spend several months here. Of course, he would have to move out of the Ritz and maybe even find a job...could Steve help with that, he wondered.

Steve's pensive mood was over and he was back to talking. His favorite topic always seemed to involve women. He told Paul that when he was onstage, he would look out in the crowd, focus on one particular lady and visualize a passionate sexual encounter right then and there. And for him, Vancouver's ladies were most open to his charms. As the city drew women from all over the country, he felt comfortable in expanding his viewpoint to include all Canadian women.

'Seems like everybody has some special philosophical message to peddle,' Paul thought. He definitely felt it wasn't something he was doing that had inspired the long winded speeches of Enrico or Steve, but Man, he'd heard a truckload and they were still coming.

Next, Steve broke down what he had discerned to be 'The Dilemma of Canadian Womenfolk.'

"You see, though the national flag is a very mellow symbol of a maple leaf, the men are into any and every sport that involves hitting and bruising - rugby, lacrosse, football, ice hockey, soccer, whatever. In between preparing for the next game or mending a broken something, they're drinking beer with the guys. This leaves their women in need of male attention. So any guy, White, Black, Asian whatever, can at least fill the void for a little while and consequently fall into *Big Fun*. Oh, Canadian men run their homes, as much as any man can believe that 'Man is King of his Domain,' but their ladies are not the type to wait at home for them to get around to dating them or even supporting them financially."

Steve continued, "People visiting Canada - tourists and even nerds - are expected to service them. And many times the women are the heartbreakers, instead of the other way around." *Sounding very much like a justification*, Steve went on, "This makes it easier to engage and disengage in relationships. Just like singing to one then moving on to the woman sitting in the chair right next to her."

Steve bragged that he was concurrently running at least four relationships, and was always looking for another. If a lady wanted to play, he would find the time. And being busted or getting caught cheating was not in his vocabulary. Each lady was led to believe that she was the one and only at that moment in time.

This sounded sort of like Enrico's philosophy. The difference was Steve needed to get inside as many as he could.

In his words, the lovemakin' was *gettin' paid*, whereas Enrico was more into the mind fuck, Paul decided. Without a pause from his dictum on women, as he focused on the glass he was holding in his hand Steve switched to another topic.

"Did you have any problems at the border getting into Canada?" questioned Steve, throwing back his third shot of Johnnie Walker Red. "The Canadian border cops think every Black Man and Longhair is trying to escape the U.S. and pollute their soil."

"Not really. In fact, the dude was very mellow," Paul recalled.

"Mellow?" Steve queried, very surprised. "More like the Gestapo, from my experiences. I have personally been detained up to two or three hours, several times. Whether it's because of my long hair or being a musician, I can't say. I have a buddy who is Black. He was born and raised in Ontario, Canada, in Toronto. They mess with him every time he crosses the border. It's like the border cops just can't accept that he's a Canadian citizen. That Black folks live here, are from here, Dig! John doesn't help things either, by directly challenging their stupid questions with arrogance and ownership of his citizenship as a proud Black Canadian. Brother loves to educate his Canadian countrymen that his family goes back at least three generations."

Steve continued, "Consider your experience at the border, a gift. Next time, brace yourself for a different kind of encounter with the Customs Folk.

"If you had a Work Visa you'd have some backup with the Pigs. Actually, gettin' one ain't that big a deal. All you need is some kind of regular gig and a house address...I mean, what did you call them? MELLOW! You will see after you been around awhile. Mark my words. The Royal Canadian Mounties can be some vicious mothers when they want to be.

Never underestimate the power of The Man.

"You should definitely think about staying awhile, Paul. I know you'll like it. And I'll help you however I can to make it happen. I came up here just looking for a new stage to perform on and found open arms. Those arms are waitin' for you too, my Good Brother."

CHAPTER 11

STEVE HAD CONVINCED PAUL TO STAY ON AND JOIN the band. It only took one jam session for the rest of the group to agree that Paul was a good fit.

Enrico and Jennifer became regular visitors at Oil Can Harry's nightclub on the nights when Paul took to the stage to perform with Steve and Ecstasy. They frequently invited Paul to parties and events around Vancouver. One night during a dinner party at their apartment, Jennifer had cornered Paul and asked him to explain how a total jock, ex-Marine could be so much into funky blues bass guitar.

"Well, my Uncle Melvin gave me my first guitar for my fourteenth birthday along with paid music lessons. He's still quite popular around the Bay Area as a jazz pianist and vocalist, but he doesn't record anymore. Initially, with keeping up my athletic endeavors and honor student status, I was pissed about the time commitment to those lessons. Then my uncle introduced me to how the bass guitars influenced the music piece. Uncle Mel was more like my big brother. Like you Jennifer, I was an only child. He was only five years older than me and sort of the renegade compared to my Dad and his four other over-achieving brothers. But when Melvin started making a little rep for himself and was always the life of every party, he was better accepted and appreciated by the family. All the other brothers are lawyers. Well, the music thing, it stuck, and I put together a little group. That's how Steve and I met. Actually we were in the same homeroom. But we only became aware of each other when we were competing with our bands in a school talent contest."

"Didn't Steve play basketball with you?" she asked.

"Yeah, but he was Junior Varsity," Paul answered quickly. "Good hands but he was a little squirt back then. Grew like a weed after graduating from high school."

"What do you like most about being a part of the band?" Jennifer continued.

"I love how the bass guitar provides the low pitched baselines and base runs in a lot of different styles of music. I mean people are raving about lead guitarists like Hendrix and Eric Clapton. Hendrix is my idol, but my first star was Larry Graham of Sly and the Family Stone. Hey, this will blow you away: Paul McCartney of the Beatles is a bass guitarist."

"Wow, I know about Larry Graham. And I know McCartney is a great lyricist and vocal artist, but I just thought the guitar was more of a stage prop," Jennifer laughed.

"Listen again to "Something" that George wrote. It's McCartney doing that fantastic guitar work on that track."

"I'll put *Abbey Road* on right now." She then embarrassed Paul by telling everyone in the room that he was going to sing for them. Having no choice in the matter, Paul proceeded to impress everyone at that party with a little vocal presentation of his favorite track.

After two nights in a row watching Jennifer come to Oil Cans by herself, Paul sat at her table between sets and asked where Enrico was. "Gone Baby. Like split the scene," she casually replied. Paul asked if they could hook up after the show. That was their beginning.

After that, Paul went all out. Picnics, walks, ice cream dates and a week later Jennifer asked him to move in with her. Paul accepted readily. He'd been living with a bunch of musicians and an assortment of other don't-give-a-fuck folks in an old house in Kitsilino. There were always dirty dishes in the sink, not to mention the toilet and shower areas were filthy.

There was never any guarantee the Chinese food or carton of milk you left in the refrigerator would still be there the next day. So Paul didn't have to think twice. Jennifer's apartment was always immaculate, and of course, the space and the view were deluxe. And using her address definitely ensured his work visa being approved. The new challenge was adjusting to living with a woman.

In the bedroom, after their second time making love, Jennifer announced, "Soldier Boy, the first thing I'm going to teach you is how to pleasure me one hundred percent of the time." Paul didn't like the nickname she'd given him, but her other nickname of choice was Hambone. Of the two, Paul definitely preferred Soldier Boy, especially in public. Also, he didn't mind the teaching sessions *at all*.

Some days she expected him to live with her and treat her as if they were married. Other times she would be gone for several days and reappear with no explanation offered. If he did ask where she'd been, she would literally scream in his face, telling him it was none of his damn business. It was her place and she made the rules.

The sex was unbelievable but never automatic. Intimacy had to be started with a seduction, a promise of adventure - not just lust but a guarantee of fulfillment. Finding just the right words was not a necessity but *absolute desire* most definitely was. You had to show her you wanted her like nothing else mattered at that moment in time. She would not be a mere sperm receptacle - a commonly shared sentiment of her girlfriends. Each and every time they had sex, they took each other to a rare and exquisite place. It felt like a new discovery every time. And she had no problem reminding him that this was Enrico's finest gift to her...the gift of who she was as a woman, a very special woman.

Paul could not deny that she had opened his mind to a higher level of pleasure and understanding of lovemaking, along with the skills she'd taught him. This alone was worth putting up with all the other stuff that she brought into the relationship. But the unpredictable nature of her daily actions was wearing him down.

Steve had turned him on to a great group of guys who played basketball every Sunday on an outdoor court at Kitsilano Beach. In turn, Paul had invited two other guys, DJ and Rich, who he'd met at the club. DJ's older brother had guest-starred a couple of times at Oil Cans. Dean Smith was big-time back in his hometown of Toronto and a personal friend of the owner of the club, who was also from Toronto.

After the games, two other Brothers would invite him, Steve, DJ, and Rich up to their place for grits and eggs, to watch some NBA action on the tube, and of course, to talk shit. The talk usually involved women. Steve would keep the guys entertained with his stories of being a close friend of Bill Graham, the producer and Fillmore Auditorium magnet, as well as the notorious Iceberg Slim, a big time pimp. Paul knew a little more about Iceberg Slim aka Robert Beck. His first book was on the reading list for the freshman Psychology 101 class: *Pimp, the Story of my Life*. As far as Paul understood, Iceberg had never pimped in San Francisco. But Steve was always entertaining and Paul never let on what he knew.

It was Roger's apartment where they'd go after 'ball and hang out. Roger was working in Vancouver for a large company based out of Chicago. This gave him cash flow and pocket change that the college students and musicians in the gathering could only dream about. Roger's roommate was 'Tater Pie.' The story was his family had nicknamed him Tater Pie because he could eat twenty sweet potato pies in one sitting. He also loved to cook and did it all - Creole, French, Italian. He was King of the Pots. Roger and Tater Pie both spent probably eighty percent of their paycheck in the many clubs and pubs around town. *Chasing the Ladies*. When at work, he was Charles Wittinham, a savvy computer programmer, in great demand. Away from work, he was Tater Pie, cock-hound extraordinaire.

Rich and DJ were on the Simon Fraser University Basketball Team and that definitely brought their basketball scrimmages to a higher level. They also raised the intellectual bar regarding current happenings in the world. But get a bunch of guys together and it all came back to street level when the conversation was about women.

"Rich, I bet there's a lot of hot sweet pussy up there at college, right?" questioned Roger.

"Yeah Bro. Lots of foxy ladies up there. But one major problem, that's all they got," answered Rich.

"Broke ass bitches," added DJ. "Ain't nothin' worse than hookin' up with someone as broke and hungry as you."

They all started laughing. The laughter took on a wilder level when Tater Pie shouted out, "Send them bitches down here to my place. Even pay y'all a finda's fee, cold cash. Tall, short, fat, no matter as long as they got a pussy."

"Tater say he be blackenin up dem ladies like the way he uses the spices on the fried fish he's so famous for," added Roger.

"I had ah litta Cutie ask me the other night, where is yo accent from?" laughed Tater. "I told her Detroit. And this ain't no accent; it's just the way we talk."

Roger chimed in, "And because he's such a freakin' genius with them new computers, nobody cares about what kinda accent he has. They just listen harder."

The room roared with laughter.

"How you enjoying yo'self Paul?" Roger called out as the laughter began to die down, "I hope Steve is sharing some of them bitches he's stickin? Word has it, ain't nobody in Vancouver doing more women than Steve!"

"Yah, Steve's the Ladies' Man and I'm only visiting his world of rock star benefits. But I'm holdin' my own," Paul replied.

"Oh, he's *holdin his own* all right," Steve spoke up. "Y'all know the Beach Towers at English Bay? His ole Lady has a penthouse suite there."

"Damn!" responded Roger and Tater. Even Rich and DJ nodded their heads in approval.

Rich and DJ joined the group most Sundays and Paul related to them more than the others. At least they had other conversations besides women and getting pussy. They both had basketball scholarships at SFU. Rich was also from San Francisco, same high school as Paul, but had played ball after Paul had already moved on to Stanford.

Tater had dictated a rule that Paul, Rich, and DJ couldn't play on the same team together. It really wasn't fair to the other guys. There were a few other competitive guys, but most of them, with the exception of Steve, were wannabes.

One Sunday morning, as Paul and DJ were putting on their sneakers waiting to get a game in, Paul asked, "So is there a story around your moniker?"

DJ broke into a slow smile. The Brother had a very mellow demeanor.

"I was a disc jockey in Toronto. Mostly played basketball, but you know my brother is the musician, Dean Smith. I was always promoting his work, playing his stuff. So someone pinned the name DJ on me and it stuck. I prefer my birth name Ralph Dubrowski. But when you're as big and Black as me, people never seemed to get comfortable with it, so I changed it to John Smith. Border cops on both sides of the U.S. and Canadian line go crazy every time I cross, with me being a Canadian citizen, born in Toronto."

Paul nodded. "Yeah. Dean Smith. Love his work. Man's tunes are uniquely him."

Steve, who was standing close by, overheard the conversation and smiled. He loved catching dudes expounding shit and not keeping things straight. "Wait a minute, is the name Dubrowski or Smith? Did your brother Dean change his name as well?" he said to DJ.

"OK, OK, so my family name is Smith, but I get a lot of mileage off the Dubrowski game.

When frequently and suspiciously asked by the authorities, "So your name is John Smith, Eh? Couldn't you have thought of a more creative name for your fake ID CARD?" I give 'em the Dubrowski story."

And again everybody was rolling with laughter.

Just as Paul was ready to fire off his own set of questions about DJ growing up Black in Canada, DJ giggled, literally giggled. A six foot six inch massive 250 pounder, giggling. Whereas most basketball players were long and lean in stature, this guy looked like a linebacker from the football team. After enjoying many a Sunday morning trying to score over him, Paul had learned to appreciate his basketball skills. Paul had promised several times to visit the campus since he'd hooked up with the Sunday morning Ball n' Grits sessions, but he had only got as far as watching one SFU vs. UBC basketball game over at the University of British Columbia campus, shortly after arriving in town.

"Know I've said it before Man, but you really need to come up to campus and check out my world one of these days," said DJ.

After the game, back at the apartment, the talk continued.

"I've been married to three Canadian women." said Tater Pie.

"Yeah, after they get their dual citizenship, the marriage somehow goes downhill." Roger offered, smiling from ear to ear.

"Are you saying them women are using your good buddy?" Steve questioned with a straight face.

"Call it what ya want." Tater Pie responded, "I was madly in love with each and every one of dem ladies."

"You think if they were not getting an American citizenship out of it, they would have married you?" Steve questioned further.

"Well, as far as I can figure," Tater said, "ta me it was always a mutual arrangement!"

The entire room roared with laughter and fist pounding.

CHAPTER 12

LATER THAT DAY, OVER DINNER AT THEIR FAVORITE fish and chips hangout, Steve asked Paul how it was going with Jennifer.

"Well," said Paul, "Jennifer has this way of flirting with whoever she pleases. We agreed the relationship would be open and initially I thought I could deal with it, but it's in my face. I know she is messing with my head. Man, she is a *master manipulator.*"

His life felt empty. Hard to believe that's what he felt. He had pockets full of money, he was living in a penthouse apartment and Jennifer was beautiful. Her latest favorite song was Peggy Lee's "Is That All There Is?" They had just seen the singer live at the Cave last week. Jennifer had dropped one of her acid bombs on him later that night in bed. "You know what Peggy Lee was singing about up there tonight?"

"She's been through a few disappointments, I guess," answered Paul.

"We seek pleasure wherever we can find it, because in the end, life is nothing more than an endless series of disappointments."

Paul recalled glibly asking, "Are you speaking of me, or life in general?"

"Life in general, I guess. I mean, did you look into the woman's eyes while she was singing? I mean we were sitting right there in the front row sipping champagne and Peggy was taking us right into her heart. Is that all there is? One heartbreak after another. But don't worry my friend, for right now, we'll just keep dancing." It was the first time Paul had witnessed real tears in her eyes. He knew there just had to be more to life than one sad story after another. He knew there was more to his future than what was happening now.

He had been raised in a family that revered education. "It's the only thing that no one and no power can take away from you," his mother would say to him every time he brought home a report card full of A's from school. He had recently felt the need to enroll in night school. He could take a foreign language or something, just to stay in the game. He made a promise to himself that he would return somewhere, to at least, complete his undergrad degree. But the immediate problem at hand was Jennifer.

Paul said to Steve, "Do you ever think that maybe what you figure is happening between you and your lady may not be where she's going with the scene?" He was asking a question he definitely knew would have a glib answer from this cockhound.

Surprisingly, instead of Steve's usual rapid-fire retort, he paused and considered his response thoughtfully. Then he replied, "Brotherman, you can analyze a situation to the nth degree and still not come up with what a woman has in her head. My dad left us when I was about seven. My mom had to switch from nestmaker to hunter *and* nester. It made her bitter. And she shared every bloody conflict and complaint she had with my old man, with *me*, every chance she got. Maybe because it was just the two of us. Maybe she just needed a sounding board. But I listened and hated my father for doing this to us. I imagined he was off somewhere living the good life. Dad tried to get back with her a few years later but Mom wouldn't take him back and so he left town…again. My mom never shared her reasons why that didn't fly. All I know is *me* getting my dad back didn't happen. I was twelve at the time. Maybe she stopped talking to me about my dad because I was looking too much like him and not like her baby boy anymore. I don't know and will never know. But what I do know is, there is no pat answer. Be in the game and enjoy the game while you can, Dig? Don't go searching for stuff that can't be found!"

What Paul couldn't man up and share with his buddy was the fact that he obviously couldn't control Jennifer. Enrico was still the ultimate man in her life and he was not Enrico. She would always know just how to make him feel like he had messed up, like it was his fault something had not turned out as planned. Paul knew Enrico would never have let that shit fly.

Jennifer was quick with her tongue and had an acid wit that could burn through whatever surface it contacted and then evaporate without any trace of malicious intent. Except of course *the damage was done*. The message imprinted. Burned down to the bone.

Though he was making good money with the band, Jennifer would not allow him to pay for anything. She had no problem reminding him and everyone else that this was what was happening. She bought him clothes and allowed him free access to the Austin-Healey - which had turned out to be hers, not Enrico's, as the man had led him to believe.

Many times Paul felt he was paying for Enrico's bad behavior or her inability to keep him. Sometimes he felt like some kind of partially trained pet. He found himself rebelling at random shit just because he didn't like her tone. She would frequently say Enrico had no problem with this or that situation. Being constantly compared to Enrico was taking its toll.

Away from the apartment, the life of a freewheeling musician was not a place for mental wellbeing either. The groupie sex was a 'Change Your Partner' dance event. Everything and anything was going down. *Sex, Drugs, and Rock 'n Roll*. No one looked out for anyone else, let alone themselves. If you were a member of the band, the girls would spread their legs and perform handstands and cartwheels. Being a celebrity of sorts, did have its privileges but Paul just couldn't get comfortable with it all. Steve fully embraced the life and literally flourished. He loved the audience and the audience loved him back. Why care who the lady was yesterday, or for that matter an hour ago? Paul found himself caring, not necessarily on a moral basis, just about the lack of personal interaction.

Almost every day Paul indulged his love for jogging or taking long walks and he played basketball at least twice a week. It was a nondescript kind of existence. The seemingly never-ending line of live women around Vancouver made his job as a musician effortless rather than *real world*. Something had to give. The universe had to get his attention and BAM...

On September 18th, Jimi Hendrix died and Sammy, the drummer from their band, OD'd and could not be revived. Joining the band on the heels of someone dying, not to mention the number of soldiers he had watched die in battle, made Khalil Gibran's words even more prophetic:

Life and death are one, even as the river and sea are one...For what is it to die but to stand naked in the wind and to melt into the sun? And what is it to cease breathing but to free the breath from its restless tides, that it may rise and expand and seek God unencumbered?...And when the earth shall claim your limbs, then shall you truly dance.

Paul still kept with him *The Prophet*, the little book his Spanish teacher from high school had given him. He found himself rereading it frequently. 'Yeah,' Paul thought further, 'but with that dance, a dance with death, there is no encore or repeat performance.' From all accounts Jimi Hendrix had been dealing with his own very 'restless tides.' Only three years had passed between Jimi rocketing to stardom at the Monterey Festival and his death at the age of 27, two months before his 28th birthday. What was ironical about Sammy's death was that he too was just shy of his 28th birthday.

Sammy had just wanted to stay high all the time. He said he felt being high made his music better. Whether it was true or not, he'd read somewhere that Miles demanded everyone performing with him had to shoot heroin to achieve the quality of play he wanted. But Ecstasy's music was nowhere near the status nor quality of Miles Davis' world. Paul stayed away from the heavy shit, as did Steve. Paul had watched firsthand too many fellow soldiers get so wasted on heroin and crap that their minds never returned to functioning right. And even if they survived *the War*, they came home with a serious monkey on their back, *a chain around their brain*, and a different kind of war to fight.

CHAPTER 13

PAUL HAD NEVER THOUGHT OF HIMSELF AS A SUPER-stitious person. But that old saying that bad luck comes in threes was working on his head. Big Tom, Oil Cans Fu Manchu bouncer, got into a motorcycle crash leaving Sammy's funeral. So there he was in a hospital bed at Vancouver General Hospital with broken femurs. With both legs in traction, he was looking like a puppet on strings with wires and pulleys going this way and that.

While waiting for the doctor to make his rounds to Big Tom's room, Mr. Bishop, the orthopedic tech, was trying to reassure the group of friends gathered around that Big Tom would be fine.

"One good thing about broken bones, doctors can fix them. Can't fix cancer, can't stop folks from getting into accidents, but we do a pretty good job of fixing bones."

Steve had brought Paul to VGH, and afterwards he dropped him back at Oil Cans and came in for a drink. He was still trying to convince Paul to come to this groupie party over in West Vancouver. "That was really some set last night, eh Paul?" said Steve.

"Eh Man, the shit is getting pretty heavy here. I feel I'm going to split soon." Paul heard these words come out of his mouth, forgetting that earlier Steve had mentioned things would be changing soon, regarding the group.

Paul was thinking more seriously about going back to college, although he did not know how Jennifer would like this plan. He was more like a house pet than an equal partner in a loving relationship.

"Say Paul, why don't you come with me tonight for a little impromptu party of sorts?" Steve continued, not acknowledging Paul. "You remember the two chicks backstage after the first set last night?"

"Vaguely," said Paul, "what about them?"

"Well Dig, Man. They got a crib over in West Vancouver and told me to come on up whenever I feel the urge."

"Well, it sounds like you're going to have some time tonight. Sounds nice Steve but *No Thanks*. I'll get a cab and scoot on back to my crib in a little bit."

Paul remembered they had talked earlier that day about Sammy's death breaking up Ecstasy. Steve and Bill had already decided to maybe do a few gigs in the owner's club in Toronto and had assumed that Paul would tag along.

"Suit yourself, Man. The ladies' folks are loaded four-forty-Z, Porsches, Mercedes. You're passing up a one-time deal. Just trying to help out a friend. Check you later, Paul."

"Okay, Steve. Later."

Paul knew all too well what was in store for Steve that night. The scene was so predictable. There would be a lot of drinking, acting stupid, more stupid horseplay, then sloppy kisses and grabbing, followed by juvenile submission to sexual acts. A weak excuse to engage in whatever freakish things that followed. Crazed out testosterone-driven drugged and drunk kids just weren't floating his boat tonight.

Being noble did have its downside, however. Choosing not to participate did nothing for his current state of being horny. Jennifer was supposedly at a family function up at Whistler.

Angie Kroener, the club owner's lady, had overheard Paul turning down Steve's party offer and invited him to join her for a shot of Scotch. She had caught Paul off guard, as he was deep into his own thoughts.

"Oh, Hi Angie." She was five feet nine inches with the proportions of a goddess.

"Paul, can't understand why a *Great Big Beautiful Man* like you would not want to join your man Steve for the groupie party?"

"Well, Sister. You are Canadian. Sometimes this place just sort of overwhelms me and I can't decide." he replied, joking around. Angie was actually half Black and half German, Canadian all the same, but very exotic looking. Her father was German-Canadian, her mother an Afro-American jazz singer who had been performing in Berlin when her parents met. They'd married and moved back to his hometown Toronto, Ontario.

Paul continued, "Maybe you can answer that better than me. When the mood hits, you go for it. Now, if you were my woman, I wouldn't be so hard up, worrying about what I was missing out on. In fact, if you were available? But I know your Old Man wouldn't dig that. If only you and Bob were not..."

Angie interrupted, "Why worry about him? I know he has a woman down in Seattle. He's probably there right now."

"Yeah," Paul leaned back into his seat with a big grin. "Well, if I had a fine woman like you, we definitely wouldn't be here right now."

"Where would we be?" said Angie.

"Well, where your thighs should be, under mine."

"Talk's cheap. Want to split now?"

"The sooner the better."

"Here are the keys to my car. You know the one. Meet you there in ten minutes." Along with her keys she gave Paul a smile like he'd never before seen from Angie, only in his dreams.

"I'm *Leavin' Right Now!*"

She and Paul had talked several times before tonight and he knew her story. After a year as a student at University of Toronto, she had been sweet-talked into coming out to the West coast with Bob who had also promised her a wedding ring as soon as they got things together with the nightclub business in Vancouver. That was four years ago. Bob was now owner of three different places, making grand theft cash, but still no ring.

Angie liked to crack everybody up telling about how her parents used to play with one another. Her mother called her dad 'Blonde Bitch' and he called her his 'Black Queen Whore.' They had died together in a car crash when Angie was eighteen.

Paul and Angie were pressing thighs and a whole lot more before her apartment door was even fully closed. The only reason I'm doing this…Bob's fucking this lady's cousin right now,' Paul rationalized. He was searching for justification for screwing his friend's woman. He hoped the rumors about Angie being a sex freak were true. Before he could conjure up more reason for enthusiasm, Angie was all over him. She had unzipped him and grabbed his manhood, inspected, approved, and was riding him like a new bicycle on Christmas morning. Now Paul was working to keep up with her.

'Oh Yes,' he began talking to himself, 'the thrust of experienced thighs. Turn her over, go deeper, dog it, she's digging this shit. Back over, lose yourself, lose yourself in that beautiful golden flesh of woman. Can't stop, you'll be sore for a week, Angie my love. This is feeling so good. Now easy, move around inside her, make her feel all of me. Help me help you take it *all*. Help me explode so hard inside you that you can't walk straight for a week. I can say without a doubt, I've truly experienced a sex goddess tonight. This is feeling so incredible. Beautiful, wonderful Angie.'

Beautiful, Beautiful Angie.

'Sure hope Bob is out the whole night. Not a nice way for a war hero to die. No pussy's worth dying over, but… guitar player shot in the ass by jealous husband, jealous cheating husband who's not even her husband! But who can feel the hurt of being cheated on unless they're guilty of the same crime? *Crazy World.*'

In the background, Jimi was playing "*Hey Joe, where you goin with that gun in your hand?*"

'Ah, I'm coming close. Yes, yes, tingle, sensate, vibrate. I wonder if she's thinking the same thing I'm thinking right now. Just how fantastic this is feeling to me.'

"Say, Angie," Paul said while falling onto his back, feeling very satisfied and pleased with his own performance.

"Yes, Baby?"

"What are you thinking about right now?"

Angie didn't hesitate a second. She grabbed him between his legs again, opened her mouth, and said, "Getting laid... some more."

CHAPTER 14

THE FOLLOWING MORNING AS PAUL WAS SITTING AT the kitchen table feeling very mellow, Jennifer returned home. Her hair was dishevelled and she looked like she'd slept on a park bench. But he knew better than to say anything for fear that her acid bomb tongue would hurl something back at him as to where *he* had spent the night, with that grin on his face so early in the morning.

'Some relationship,' Paul mused to himself, not feeling proud of the current situation, both of them partying in different directions. He had just gotten off the phone with Steve who'd talked nonstop, giving every detail of last night's encounter with the two young ladies he had played with.

"Wow, that Steve is really something else!" he said, trying to start a normal conversation with Jennifer.

"Yes," said Jennifer, "a different girl every night for that randy fellow."

"What's wrong with that? He seems to be enjoying himself."

"So, you think he's enjoying himself, eh? According to Steve, he hates himself. Says he just can't find the right one. Did you two find some action while I was away?"

Paul wasn't expecting that question and attempted to avert it by focusing on the recurring pattern of her continually

91

working Steve into their conversations lately. He usually ignored it, but he'd stored the information just for a time like now when he could use it to take the attention off himself. For some reason, she seemed to be fonder of Steve these days. Not so critical, but had avoided explaining why. And until now he hadn't felt like digging any further.

"Steve Says. Steve Says. You did the Astrological Chart on him, didn't you?" Paul said angrily. "That's why you think you know so much about Steve and how Steve feels."

"Well, he was looking for you the other day and I invited him up for tea. You know he's a Scorpio and they often have difficulties controlling their physical needs. They are all about intensity and contradictions, the most misunderstood of all the signs. I did his reading while he was here. I mentioned it to you. You probably don't remember. You never listen to what I'm saying, most of the time. Oh forget it, Paul," said Jennifer, as she turned away.

"Forget what? What's been troubling you lately? And don't give me none of that *astrology crap* either," Paul continued in an aggressive tone. Her usual response would be to quote his morning horoscope for Gemini, his sign, and explain his mood from that perspective. And many times she was right on target. Recently he'd found himself consulting the morning paper for his daily reading or thumbing through the huge book on the coffee table that contained anything and everything one would want to know about celestial observations and terrestrial events within the House of Astrology.

"Astrology Crap? You're forever jumping to conclusions, always thinking you know so damn much," she fired back.

"Look, Jennifer," Paul said, very loudly. "I'm sick and tired of you and your astrological explanations for everything. I'm Paul Marshall and you're Jennifer McAuley, right? Go play your morning paper horoscope game with someone else and talk straight up for once!" He got up from the table and walked out of the room.

Jennifer followed him. "Where are you running to, Soldier Boy? You started this. Afraid I might lose my temper and say something about your trifling life? How well you follow the duality of the Gemini personality. You have a problem finishing what you started. You're running off in a new direction and chasing a new idea every freakin' week. One day music, the next day sports. Have you committed to anything yet? We've talked about your time in 'Nam, after you were shot, your near-death experience. And how you could never be the person you were before that happened. But nothing happened in that accident that wasn't already going on... scrambled eggs before, scrambled eggs up there now."

"*WHAT??* Who appointed you Master Shrink?"

"I don't need any damn degree to see through your weak-ass shit. Oh, Yeah. Steve told me a lot about you. Who else do you talk to? And when were you going to tell me about the band splitting up?" She caught herself and walked back into the kitchen. She hadn't meant to express her displeasure that he shared things with Steve and not with her. She was so unhappy that their only meaningful communication was happening between the sheets. But that was too important a conversation to get into now, and so was the news of Ecstasy breaking up.

"Shut up, Dammit! Jennifer, I said shut your damn mouth up. Every motherfucking time I turn around, you got your damn mouth open. You think you know so damn much - think I know so damn little? Well, let me be the first to tell you, Bitch. You ain't shit! I know enough to know that you ain't got much of a game plan either. You'll never stop sucking your parents' tits - your mamma's and daddy's tits."

Jennifer said with authority, "And who's been supporting your ass for the past six months?? That's the real reason you wanted me. Money. Yeah, Steve told me about you bragging the other day how good you got it here. Come on, Paul, tell me to my face. And when were you going to tell me the band was splitting up?"

"Dammit, I'll murder him!" exclaimed Paul. Now he was really angry. He knew Steve all too well. He was getting into her head first and his next move would be into her panties. Why else would he have told her about Ecstasy and the rest!

"Murder who, BigMan? Steve or yourself? Of course, you couldn't murder yourself because you don't even know who you are or where you're going."

Paul turned around furiously and raised his arm to knock Jennifer down with an open hand. He immediately drew his hand back. He didn't want to do that. He had never hit a woman in his life. In fact, he hated to see or hear about men who beat up on women. That wasn't his style. 'What is happening here?' he asked himself. He looked at her. 'Is she orchestrating this scene? Is this how Enrico controlled her, by physically dominating her? This ain't me. Not Paul Marshall.'

Yeah. Paul thought he'd found part of the answer. "So this was how Enrico controlled your crazy ass?"

"Enrico never laid a hand on me. He would kick your ass right this minute if he saw you lifting your arm to hit a woman. He didn't have to physically dominate. *Power of the Mind* was his thing!" screamed Jennifer. She looked at him defiantly. "Someday you may understand what Enrico and I shared. And if you even fathomed my man would use his fist to control any situation, you surely missed the boat on the wisdom he tried to gift you."

Paul felt so confused with anger and compassion brewing equally in his head toward Jennifer. He wanted put his arms around her and just hold her for a moment. Yet he felt betrayed by her forging a relationship with Steve. Then again, the rules that made it easy to party with a groupie or two did not exclude anyone. There was nothing more that could be said. He stormed out of the apartment.

He found himself in his usual place of refuge...walking the Sea Wall of Stanley Park. His preference was to jog, but there was a blanket of heavy fog this morning. Visibility was no more than a few feet around him and it felt real good. He took a few deep breaths and his head started to clear. The rest of the world disappeared. It was just him. He could escape back to his preteen years...delivering the morning *Chronicle* on his paper route up and down the hills of San Francisco. Of course, it was foggy or overcast seventy percent of the year in the Oceanview and Ingleside districts. The fog felt like home, like the friend he needed to embrace him, after the ugly scene he'd just left.

Just like the letters that were never sent to JoAnn, his communication with Jennifer was lacking. With Ecstasy dissolving, Jennifer was probably feeling she was about to be abandoned, again, this time by him. Paul knew he was wrong in not sharing the news of the band with her.

But the bottom line was that living the way he was living was becoming more and more problematic. Life was not supposed to be what Peggy Lee sang of, one disappointment after another. *Not his life.*

It was time to part ways. It would be hard giving up Jennifer's nest. But Mama J's boot was still being felt on his behind. If he stayed on after this last battle, it would be worse than Virginia Woolf's wrathful ways. Jennifer was the Queen of Mind Games, schooled by a Master of the Game. He felt there was no alternative but to split with her right now and get out of this toxic place they were in.

CHAPTER 15

PAUL CHECKED INTO THE LOCAL YMCA. THE NEXT morning he saw a poster on the bulletin board about a student group at SFU trying to raise money for Angela Davis and the Black Panthers. He was even more impressed to learn that the principal student organizers were his two buddies from the Sunday morning Ball 'n Grits. DJ and Rich had asked him more than a few times to come up to the campus and hang out. He decided to check them out. Simon Fraser Campus, Burnaby Mountain, Black Students' Union Office.

The guys were boasting they had chartered the first Black Students' Union in Canada, although a group in Montreal were touting the same accomplishment according to an article he'd read earlier that day. Much of the free reading material at the Y was from campuses, both local and around the country. Apparently, there was a lot of student unrest with a group in Montreal who were citing allegiance to the Black Panthers organization in the U.S. They called themselves the FLQ - Freedom Liberation group of Quebec.

It was a straight shot ride up Hastings Street, then another bus up Burnaby Mountain to that concrete structure he'd spotted while having drinks with Steve that day. The world famous architecture of Simon Fraser University sat on the top of a mountain where his homeboys reigned.

The campus of the University of British Columbia, the other older university in Vancouver, was very similar to the University of California with old brick buildings, rolling green lawns and trees. He had visited UBC a couple of times, as it was just up from Kitsilano where he'd lived before moving in with Jennifer. The SFU campus was different, all modern and concrete. As the bus climbed higher and higher up, he felt an even greater admiration for the college kids who were getting off this isolated mountain campus to start breakfast programs and tutorial workshops for needy children in local communities. Being up and away from everything, the school was separated from the city by acres of nature.

The bus dropped off the passengers at a place called the Rotunda that looked like the entrance to a spaceship, like something out of a *Star Trek* episode. The Rotunda housed most of the Student Offices including the Black Students' Union.

DJ was waiting for him as he'd promised on the phone. His tour started at a large covered mall-like area. DJ showed him the library on the left and to the right a place they called The Theatre. With pride, DJ explained that free noon movies were shown here as well as student-produced plays. He and Rich were active in the student stage productions. Entertainers like Oscar Peterson and Gordon Lightfoot performed free concerts at this venue also. Next to The Theatre were areas with chairs and desks that faced glass walls looking down at the spectacular view of the surrounding forest and municipalities.

"Hey DJ," asked Paul, "Can we see New Westminster from here? I shared some hospital space with a Canadian kid from New Westminster back in Vietnam."

"Man, you can see all the way to Washington State from here. New West would be to the south and east just below us. I actually took a course last year called *The Architecture of Arthur Erickson*," said DJ. "He was the dude that designed SFU. It opened in 1965."

Paul could easily appreciate the transition from the wooded slopes to the cement majesty this guy Erickson had envisioned. The place was a maze of covered walkways, landscaping, and outdoor sculptures. Concrete and glass in juxtaposition with nature. Equally amazing was that it had another side to it, a *Giant Spaceship for Higher Intelligence*, just outside the urban beauty of Vancouver.

"You can really feel trapped up here." DJ went on, never at a loss for words. "When the sun is out, it's a wonderful thing. But on a cold foggy day, all these gray concrete walls make it feel like a prison. Especially when you ain't got wheels or a ride to get off the mountain. Erickson worked with a super team and amazingly built this sucker in only a couple of years. So of course, there are a few structural problems, like *big time* building leakage. Just last year they were getting a better handle on it. Those of us who live on campus have learned to deal with it. But that's what these construction zones and detours are all about, shoring up shit.

"For you dudes from San Francisco, the fog won't bother you much. At least that's what Rich preaches. There he is now. Rich! Rich, over here, Man. Look who made it up the hill!" shouted DJ.

Rich came over. The two men embraced and did the full Brother clasp ritual. "You know I missed breaking your scoring record when I graduated from our high school by twenty freakin' points."

"Our Sunday get-togethers were fun, but I never really got a chance to rap with you guys the way I wanted. Then when your Basketball season started, we never saw you." Paul said. "I've been meaning to ask you why you chose to take a basketball scholarship up here and not some of the other awesome places that wanted to recruit you back home."

Rich replied, "I dig where ya comin' from and glad you made the trip up here. Getting back to your question, I wanted to continue as a student athlete...not just an athlete performing for the college. You know, using basketball to pay for my degree. Student first, Athlete second is the deal at SFU. And besides, I had this problem with our coach. What an ass. If it had been left up to him, I wouldn't have gotten *this* spot. And the coach here ain't much different. At least here, I have the opportunity to accomplish my goal of getting a degree.

But get this: when the alumni here at SFU found out that Coach K went down to the States and brought back three Brothers and a Jewish kid...Assholes rearranged the scholarship deal. Like no stipends, mandatory jobs for pocket money. Only tuition and books were covered. All the world travel and awesome game schedules were taken off the table. But as far as I'm concerned it actually worked out for the better. I really feel I'm earning my stay here. And being able to focus on my studies is getting me what I wanted out of the deal."

Naively, Paul wondered, "You mean Coach Thomas was like that? I always thought he was a righteous dude."

"Man, it was Coach T blocking all my other scholarship offers except for this place which could be compared to the Foreign Legend, that's how Racist 'muthers work. Coach couldn't snuff me out totally, so he limited my options. Only he didn't realize that when Coach K laid out the academic advantages, *it was what I needed to hear.*" Rich's voice had gone up a few decibels so he took a breath and lowered it.

"Dude, you were the exception...you were not considered one of the Brothers going for a scholarship...remember Stanford had you committed in your sophomore year of high school. For the rest of us, Coach Thomas fucked with our minds, our futures. He never let us know until the very last moment if a college was interested in offering a scholarship. You know that the interested colleges usually come through the coaching office, Right? It's the coaches who tells them if you're a good prospect, whether you're coachable, have the right attitude to make it to the next level. All that stuff. It was the talk between the coaches, that determined if the school would follow through with an offer or not. My parents couldn't afford to pay for college tuition. I choose the high school we went to and had to bus across town every day, hoping for a better chance at a scholarship.

"When I left for Canada my Dad gave me the family car, a 1964 Ford Galaxy. Think about it, Man. They wanted me to feel as comfortable and entitled as the rest of the kids in school. They were one hundred percent supportive of what I was doing and all I had to do was bring home that college degree. And that's what I'm here to do.

"I lost contact with the Bay Area after I came up here. I mean I'm still very much in touch with my family, but my real job is getting an education and going as far as I can with the opportunities that will come my way. I *will* make my family proud.

"You didn't need an athletic ticket to college...I loved that about you. Like watching Willie Mays or some other star Black athlete, you inspired us. We're from the same city but completely different worlds." Rich continued, "Shit, you're as close to Black Royalty as anyone can get. It is no secret your Dad's firm was right there with all the other movers and shakers. I've seen some strange things but I was shocked to see YOU on that stage at Oil Cans...rocking out in Vancouver Canada? Far Fucking Out!"

The conversation paused for a minute as a group of girls from the Field Hockey team walked by in their short skirt uniforms showing off well-defined thighs. The three of them watched as the team passed by their table in the school cafeteria.

Then Rich continued, "I'm just about to finish my psychology degree, then onto a doctorate specializing in sports motivation. Who knows where it will take me. Maybe business or advertising. Sounds plastic, commercial maybe, but I'll need to find me a good paying job when all is said and done. One day, what I really want to do is teach. I want to be like an awesome college professor, turning on all those wonderful hungry minds that arrive searching for intellectual enlightenment and a better world. But I'm thinking I may need some work experience before I'm credible enough to *inspire*, maybe write a book or two. Simon Fraser has been a righteous place to start my ultimate dream to be a motivational speaker, Dig?"

Paul listened to Rich's passion and determination and envied his quest. Funny how things go full circle. In high school, it was Rich doing the envying, and now it was the reverse.

Paul knew he needed to change his direction in life. But how? He was at a loss. In a rather absentminded manner - not from lack of interest, but from plain envy that this guy had such clear focus and direction - he heard himself say, "San

Francisco might as well be on another planet in my mind right now. I came up to campus 'cause I heard you guys have your shit together. I need to get my shit together. No more Oil Can Harry's. The group split up. I'm impressed with the big waves you brothers are making with your 'Free Angela Campaign' and running the school programs in the Native American and West Indian communities. All that along with completing your college degrees. Awesome. Look, I'm not wanting to sign up or anything, but *I need to know* you guys. Listen to some meaningful shit for a change."

DJ spoke out, "It's not that we got our shit more together than other people up here. It's just that we takes the time to make time. Dig? I mean, like, if we can't do it for ourselves as a people, who can? As a Black Canadian, I feel even more compelled to be out there, representing in the communities. Seems like the West Indian Brothers get all the attention for bettering political awareness here in Canada."

"No, wait a minute," said Paul, "I was expecting to hear this whole rap about Brotherhood and Revolution, but I like your game. And DJ, you're a Sociology Major on the way to Law School, Right? Don't get many socially conscious talks down at Oil Cans. This is more *real talk* than I heard in a while." laughed Paul.

Rich slumped down in his chair and reflected on his conversation with Paul. Being in the upper level classes of his psychology major, he was constantly identifying particular patterns of human behavior that previously had no significance to him. Now he had to fight 'labeling' people even after brief encounters. However, Rich had seen the problems Paul was dealing with, in many kids coming from his same socioeconomic background. Kids from affluent families who were thriving in a White society that seemingly accepted and embraced them, yet never gave them the feeling of full membership - simply because of the color of their skin. Other Blacks accepted them as future leaders of the community, but these kids had no understanding of what it was to be dependent on the government for subsidized living facilities, food stamps, menial jobs, and substandard educational opportunities. On top of all of that, they also had to deal with an ever-present fear of merciless predators as in street thugs, crooked cops, and plain old institutional roadblocks.

Paul and other well-to-do Black folks were saddled with something called cognitive dissonance, when two conflicting beliefs are held simultaneously. First, they were raised to believe that they were better than others of their race but not quite as good as a White person. *Black means step back and White means Shining Light*. Secondly, with the emergence of Black Awareness and Black Power, the same people advising them to disassociate with their race were now saying the opposite. *It's cool to be Black*. Be proud of your darker skin. Cognitive Dissonance.

The Black Canadians did not seem to have the same dissonance problem in believing all Blacks were limited by the color of their skin. Instead, they seemed to have a strange sense of comfort within their community while ignoring outside negativity. This level of comfort made them less likely to challenge the powers that be and more likely to identify with others who were less fortunate. For the most part, *being better off* was enough to strive for.

With this knowledge and insight, Rich had learned to keep his thoughts to himself. No use opening up more shit that really had no immediate solution.

Rich moved to make the conversation a little less heavy for the moment and said, "Aside from all that, we go everywhere we can to meet new ladies. Only small fish up here on campus. Nice hooking up with ladies with real jobs, making their own way in life, not wannabes like us. Say Blood, why don't you come with us to our crib? We got some nice stuff just came in! And we scored a really nice apartment here on campus in the Graduate Students' living facilities."

"Beautiful," said Paul. "Let's get over there right now."

CHAPTER 16

THE LOUIS RIEL GRADUATE STUDENT APARTMENTS was a short ten minute walk from the cafeteria, pass the Rotunda. They passed the Athletic Complex that housed an Olympic-sized swimming pool at one end and basketball courts at the other. The building looked about five storeys high. Paul was told that the coaching offices, weight and fitness rooms, showers, and equipment facilities were between and below. They passed the Men's and Women's Dorms. Although the guys were still undergrads they shared an apartment with a grad student named Ross, but their roommate was seldom there. He was in a serious relationship and more or less living with his lady.

As they entered the apartment, he thought to himself how small the place looked. The entire four rooms - bedroom, bathroom, kitchen, and living room - could have fit into Jennifer's living room. This living room had a kitchen table and chairs, an old couch, and a mattress in one corner where DJ said he slept about eighty percent of the time. Ross and Rich had beds, which DJ felt was reasonable since they paid the rent. But what they did have that made it more livable and seem much bigger was a huge window with the same view as seen from the theater complex - hill after hill of forests dotted with residential areas. Way off in the distance was a snow-covered mountain, standing alone, the magnificent Mount Baker. The guys told him that the mountain was located in Washington State, just across the U.S. border.

Paul made himself comfortable on the couch opposite the window as DJ plunked down on his bed next to the stereo and record collection. He immediately threw on his brother's latest album, a folksy, jazzy infusion of Dean Smith's very unique voice. Dean had been well-received at Oil Cans last month, Paul remembered.

"You know," said Rich, "you know Man, DJ saved my sanity."

"What do you mean by that?" Paul asked.

Rich said, "When I first came to Canada and looked around and saw no Black People or very few people of color, I began feeling sorry for myself. I felt like people had me under a microscope, studying me because I was a new phenomenon. Student athletes interested in the community didn't seem to exist. Either you worked in the community, or you belonged on campus. Like oil and water. And then I met this hip dude from the East Coast." He laughed as he exhaled the pungent smelling smoke from the water pipe that was sitting on one of the two wooden crates being used as coffee tables in the middle of the room.

DJ laughed too as he flipped through the records. "Say Rich, is Ross back from his field trip with the conservation group yet?"

"Don't think so." Rich turned to Paul and explained: "Ross is a teaching assistant and he's up at this fish hatchery doing some research pertaining to his thesis."

Paul took a hit and instantly felt his brain and body sink deeper into the couch. As he listened, it seemed like DJ and Rich were becoming increasingly animated and energized and even more articulate as they imbibed.

Paul wondered outloud, "How many Brothers up here?"

DJ said, "Man, we never count up here. I mean, maybe they do, but not as seriously as they do down South," He concluded, laughing to himself. "Let's see, Canada is part of the British Empire and they gave Black folks their freedom from slavery about thirty years before Lincoln did his thing for the

United States. So folks been tricklin' up here for quite a while now just blending in or at least trying to blend. But I don't believe we have ever been over five percent of the total population. Kinda gives credence to some sort of conspiracy theory. The Black population in the U.S. has never been over ten to twelve percent. What's that about? We've never claimed sufficient numbers or gotten organized enough to gain the power necessary to even be considered a political threat up here. On campus there's about twenty or so Black Canadians but many more West Indians and Africans than Black Canadians. Then there are a few Brothers from Europe and about 10 or so U.S. Brothers."

Paul said, "The thing that really trips me out is lots of Cats up here in Canada wanna tell me all about how the people here are not heavily racist. They say the Black-White thing ain't here like it is in the States. Brother, what is racism? Somebody better clue these Negroes in on the subject. Racism is also about keeping the number of Blacks in Canada in a confused state. Just because they, meaning Black Canadians are so called *blending*, it doesn't mean they're getting better jobs or not experiencing random racial assaults, like everywhere else on this planet. How many fair-skinned Negroes have been allowed to ditch their ethnic backgrounds and are now passing for White? So many subtle ways to keep the numbers down. Strength is found in numbers. How does one control an entire race of people totalling five percent without some form of *Racist Manipulation?*"

Paul added, "One of my take home lessons from the War was that all them young soldiers dying in 'Nam won't be making no babies to add to the population numbers. Not to mention all the Brothers rotting in jails stateside. Think of *that* as a form of racist manipulation as well. So vicious and effective was the death toll on Blacks, nobody cared about the collateral loss of young White men dying in 'Nam along with them. During my tour, it was like the Viet Cong had really decided to kick our asses out of Southeast Asia with the TET Offensive. Russian guns and other weapons of war were turning up everywhere we went!"

Paul became slightly distracted when he noticed the two-foot poster of Jane Fonda in her Barbarella outfit, looking ever so sexy, hanging on the wall over the stereo. 'Must belong to the roommate,' he thought. Paul wanted to rant further about Jane's dealings with the Black Panthers, but this conversation was really about racism in Canada right now, not the Panthers. Staying focused on the present conversation and not getting back to Roger and Tater talk was why he had come up to campus. He was proud he still had the wherewithal to recognize this, even in his current state of mind fog from the Smoke.

"Ain't nothin' to wonder about. It's here," answered Rich. "I know you were listening to what was said about rearranging the scholarship agreement after the alumni didn't like Coach bringing Black faces and a Jew up here to play ball for the school. I don't feel entirely appreciated for my contribution to the Basketball clinics we are mandated to run on Saturdays for the athletic department and stuff, but it's part of the job that came with the scholarship package. But on the upside of it, think about it. We our exposing those young kids to Black people on a *realtime* basis. That has to be the *true value* of our presence here."

"Hey, Paul," said DJ in a thick voice, "are you trying to hip us to the fact that you are revolutionary? A rebel with a pick? Your bass guitar. Yeah, ready to *off* a bunch of racist Canadians, Jimi Hendrix, wah wah style."

Paul remained serious. "Well, check it out, Brotherman. I have seen enough of you Canadian dudes to know that *the man* knows he has you all in his back pocket with your white pussy fixation and happy to be a part of the British Commonwealth crap."

"Now, you just wait one goddamn minute," said DJ, rising to his full six feet six inch frame. "Shit! You fuckin niggers come up here after having snatched a few white boys' lunch bags, have a few so-called race riots, preachin' all this black unity and togetherness shit, then come here and play closet niggers. You know, like the niggers who eat their watermelons in the closet so no one can see that ain't nothin changed. Preachin' *Blacker than Thou* in the streets then being at home with their White woman and telling their babies to think 'white.' Like people can't see through that bull. Talkin' but doin' nothin' different."

Anger dissipated and mellowness returning, DJ sat down and leaned back. "Yeah, it hurt the first time I was called a nigger, but it came from jealous assholes who wanted to be me, Dig. My sense of self has always been solid, thanks to my mama. But I bet you never had your cows poisoned by the local KKK, or actually saw a cross being burnt in your hometown. Not to mention on your front lawn.

"And as for 'white pussy' shit. You wanna tell me how many niggers come up here every weekend from your country and blow that much cash on bitches that we wouldn't even look at, just to say they got some White Ass?

"Tater Pie is an excellent example of what we are talking about. During the day he's a respected computer specialist; at night, he's doing anything and everything to find his True Love. He calls it *love*, but I call it a lifetime infatuation with wanting to service and please Miss Anne, the plantation mistress. Niggas are still back on the plantation. Even here in Canada. The man has found himself a heaven, so to speak, where white bitches ain't artificially made fearful of his black skin. He gets to show his interest and the ladies respond. He isn't concerned about being used or taken advantage of because he is getting what he needs, to be accepted as a *man*. Not a White man or a Black man, but a man with something they want, whatever that may be, Dig? So you can call it a 'white pussy fixation,' but I call it another fucked up brother living out his fantasy in Canada."

Rich, rather agitated, jumped in, "I've been here for damn near three years now; know how many arguments just like this one I've listened to? The Africans think they have a patent on Black because they're from the Motherland. The Brothers from the States say they're the True Black Experience because of the slavery thing. The West Indians feel they have an upper hand on Blackness because they've been governing themselves with the advantage of the Queen's English and superiority crap. All shaking hands and hugging each other one minute then stabbing each other in the back the next."

The talk had started to feel like a *tag team* kinda deal to Paul in his stoned condition. He was just trying to keep up, but he knew he was mentally out of shape.

Rich carried on, "You know, Paul, when we were in the early stages of establishing a Black Students' Union here on campus, nobody could agree on a statement of unity. The Canadian Brothers, for the most part, thought we were all crazy for escaping unhappy environments only to spend a bunch of time criticizing Canadian life after we settled here. They have integrated so deeply they don't even know what Blackness is! They'd lost the meaning of BROTHERHOOD."

Then DJ jumped back in, "There was one thing that brought us all together, no matter where we came from. It was asking the question 'Where were you when someone called you a Nigger...the first time?' Everyone, no matter their circumstance, had a story about unexpectedly being called a Nigga by a white person with an intensity they would never forget. Be it in Africa, the West Indies, or downtown Chicago. And that, my friend, was why we needed a Black Students' Union. 'Cause there had to be *one* place on campus you could rest assured that no one in the room was thinking maliciously about the color of your skin." DJ added, "Whether it was true or not, at least in theory, the Student Union is *our* house on campus, and Rich and I put it together."

"I ain't Tommin you, Blood. Lots of ugly Crackers, but there are lots of ugly Black folks as well. You been here damn near a year, in beautiful downtown Vancouver. After seeing just *the night life people*, you want to come down on all Canadian Brothers?" Rich challenged Paul.

"Well," said Paul, as he got up to stretch, "if I sort of jumped the gun, it's just that I get so damn tired of people in general, Dig? That's what being a musician is all about. We just tune it all out and the band plays on."

Rich returned the conversation to the subject at hand: "The truth is, the Man got us so hiked up on hate, the true Brotherly love thing gets sidelined somewhere. We gotta just learn how *to Live for Love* Man, Dig?"

"Paul, I am Canadian," said DJ. "I have listened to a lot of shit through my time, and when I went to 'Frisco last year, I was extremely disappointed. So what puts you in a position to criticize all Canadian Blacks? Tell me Man, Why? How many Black folks do you really trust coming from your privileged background? I remember your boy Steve saying your Daddy is prominent in politics. The politicians are only out for themselves, all politicians, as far as I see it. So many poor folks have caught so much hell all their lives, they can't see straight anymore, just wanna be left alone. We are here at the university *growing* mentally and spiritually. That's where education takes you. We are taking in as much as there is to take in. And what I see is what Malcolm X came to see, it's a world dilemma. *RACISM IS A WORLD DILEMMA*.

"Governments five thousand miles from here ain't no different than right here on home ground. Control the people and you control their tomorrow. *That's just the way of the world and there's no simple answer.*" DJ shifted on his mattress. "Education is the mighty weapon. Machiavelli, Shakespeare, Gandhi, Frantz Fanon, they be speaking and writing *the truth*; it's all there. Somewhere it has been documented in a book. Only problem is most people stop reading when they get to the place in the book they thought they were looking for. Then they skip the rest of the pages and close the book. So their education is compromised."

Rich spoke up, "*My Man is preachin' the Truth*; think about it. Professors give you this big ass reading list, then penalize the student for not coming up with what they personally wanted you to find in the assignment. How many times does a professor objectively want the full text dissected? I mean, shouldn't there be credit given to those who actually read the entire material assigned and formed some questions as a result of all that reading and thinking? Got to another level of understanding from where they started the assignment? Hell No. You can buy an 'A' essay from three years back, or get an 'A' today by simply locking in on what the professor wants to hear. What kind of shit is that? Your degree at graduation apparently only verifies that you have been a good listener, not that you sought answers to questions that were never before asked."

Paul looked out the window. He had never gone as deep as these Brothers in thinking about the content in a book. Man, it felt good to use his brain again, even if it was presently foggy. Now he had to consider not only returning to college but getting something meaningful out of it, as well.

Was this the reason why he felt he had to change the direction he was traveling? His eyes drifted back to the view outside. He meant no disrespect to the conversation he'd instigated. He was simply getting overloaded - brain wise and chemically.

He flashed back to his plane ride home from 'Nam when he had first resolved that he would seriously pursue a law degree and then decided against it because it was a dream belonging to other people, not his own dream. Obviously he was looking for answers, searching for clues as to where he was moving next. He needed some place new to reflect on his present space. The military life? Gone. Life in the fast lane of entertainment? Gone. Where to next?

CHAPTER 17

"SAY MAN, HAVE YOU DUDES EVER BEEN OVER TO THE Island?" asked Paul.

"Vancouver Island? Yeah, Man..quite a few times," Rich said.

DJ added, "I lived near the University there for nearly four months."

"Sounds like a nice place to visit. Think that's what I'll do."

"When?" they asked in unison.

"Probably tomorrow," Paul replied.

"Well," said DJ, "here's a number to buzz when you get there...a partner of mine from Toronto. Kevin's a real together dude, big house, probably put you up for a couple of days. Say Man, don't you have to clear it with anybody? You've been here for a while. Don't you have any ties?"

"No ties, Man," said Paul in a very distant tone. "Just give me that number and I'll be on my way tomorrow."

"Say Paul," Rich spoke up, "what are you doing tonight, besides packing up for your Island trek?"

"What ya got in mind?"

"Well, I have this unofficial gig with the SFU student newspaper reporting and interviewing celebrities coming through Vancouver. DJ usually rides shotgun, but tonight he's got a hot date, some chick downtown named Angie. Richie Havens is in town tonight. Wanna come with me?"

"Wow, Richie Havens' in town and DJ's goin' to miss the happenins' for a chick? Must be *some* lady." Paul said. It did cross Paul's mind that DJ's hot date and the Angie he knew were one and the same. But he simply shrugged his shoulders, as in more power to the Brother. DJ may be in for a serious treat.

DJ came back into the room from the kitchen and commented, "What Rich ain't telling you is it's not definite he will be able to talk his way backstage, but I got a definite thing happening with this woman. And if you saw her, you would make the same choice."

Paul wanted to ask DJ straight up if the Angie he was planning to see was Angie Kroner from Oil Can Harry's, but what difference did it make? Just chalk it up to another reason to get away from the downtown scene.

Rich was driving the same Ford Galaxy his parents had given him, royal blue and big. Paul made him stop for gas and his student friend didn't decline the offer. They drove downtown to Granville Street and the Yale Hotel where the Havens' Show was happening that night.

Vancouver was such a mellow town. Rich's glibness got them to the backdoor, then the security guard recognized Paul from Oil Cans and ushered them through without a hitch.

A while later, Paul found himself in the backstage area listening to the incomparable Richie Havens sing Bob Dylan's "Just Like a Woman." The song was so appropriate for Paul as he thought, 'these lyrics could have been written about Jennifer.' He looked out into the audience and imagined himself as one of the musicians. With Steve's group, they had never ventured out of Vancouver. For Havens, the audience was the *world*. His thoughts and reality came crashing together as he spotted two familiar people sitting in the front row, kissing and hugging like teenagers on a date. Steve and Jennifer. Paul immediately flashed back to those prophetic words said by his 'best pal' not so long ago: *Be careful: not all who seem to be your Brother are really looking out for you!!!* Paul shrugged his shoulders and reaffirmed that he'd made the right decision in moving on.

Havens did grant Rich an interview for the *The Peak*.

The first question Rich posed was, "Could you discuss your purpose or goal when performing?"

"I see myself not in show business but in the *communications business*," Havens replied. "If people would take time to listen to one another they'd realize their problems are no different than those of the person next to them. Music can help all of us communicate better by appreciating what the music is speaking to, Dig?" Havens' face was very matter of fact, as was his tone, as if he'd said this many times before.

"I read you started out in New York?" Rich asked.

"I actually grew up on an Indian reservation on Long Island. My father was from the Blackfoot Tribe and my mom came from the British West Indies. I was into gospel music as a child then found myself at home in Greenwich Village. We were Beatniks back then. Writing poetry, listening to folk music, and eventually I picked up a guitar. You know it was Bob Dylan who gave me my first contract."

"So that's how you got the exclusive on "Just Like a Woman?" Rich continued.

"Right On Man, and of course you know we just released "Something Else Again" which is doing so well that people are making *Mixed Bag* popular again."

"You mentioned you were of First Nations descent, as they prefer to be called up here in Canada. Do you have any time in your schedule to come to a community center with me and talk about your Native American roots?" Rich queried.

"Brother, I would love to! We have two more shows before leaving town. How about tomorrow around noon? We're staying at the Georgia Hotel."

Havens had lit up like a Christmas tree. He was so genuine and down to earth. Paul was impressed with both of them. Rich had real interviewing skills that had opened the Man right up. He had taken Havens from giving pat answers to 'asked before' interview questions to zoning in on the man's *humanity*.

Havens then turned to Paul and asked him, "Were you born on the cusp?"

Paul did not follow him at first. Then he recalled Jennifer's obsession, and figured out that Havens was referring to the Zodiac and being born around the beginning or end of a particular sign. Paul answered affirmatively.

Richie responded that he had a similar birth date. "We are gifted people. We are blessed with the wisdom of two houses of the Zodiac. Use your gift wisely!"

Paul shot back, "But I feel stuck in the middle, sitting on the fence. I have all this knowledge inside that needs to be developed before it can benefit anyone."

"And you feel you are the first person on this planet that has ever faced that *dilemma?*" Havens asked. "If you feel that way, keep the backup job with the band. But if you can take the heat of the spotlight alone, there's a whole new world waiting to embrace you and applaud your courage." Paul realized that Havens thought he was still in the band.

"So I got another set. Will I see the two of you tomorrow?" Richie called over his shoulder as he was turning to walk away.

"Ah, I'm moving on to Vancouver Island," Paul said with remorse. It would have been nice to rap more about guitar playing and the world stage, Woodstock, and such. But he was more tripped out over Steve and Jennifer in the audience. He felt he'd known both of them well, but here they were acting like they'd been together longer than the week he'd been away from the apartment. Ah, the long arm of betrayal. That scene was *over*, he resolved, and so passing up a chance to hang out with one of his idols was just another sacrifice he was willing to make to find his *New Road*.

Paul and Rich left with their brains on fire from those words of the *Man*, Richie Havens.

CHAPTER 18

THE FERRY RIDE ACROSS TO THE ISLAND WAS ENJOY-able. It was a gorgeous day so he went up to the top deck and sat with his back against the cabin, soaking in the sun. Not far away, a group of six hippies sat in a circle. One of the guys strummed a guitar and the rest hummed or sang in an unstructured manner, free flow style. Their music created a mellow vibe as the huge boat seemed to weave in and out through a series of islands, big and small.

He found the dude Kevin's house without a hitch, even though the old mansion was virtually unseen from the road behind a heavily landscaped but badly overgrown wall of green.

"You sure it's cool for me to cop a few nights here, Man?"

"Ride On, Brother," said Kevin, shaking his big red mop of a head. "DJ and I help each other out all the time, no problem."

"Yes, well, I only intend to be on the Island long enough to see what there is to see."

"Ah Man, that's no problem," said Kevin. "In fact, there are a bunch of friends leaving next Monday for Campbell River."

"Well, I had in mind just to trip by myself."

"Oh Yeah. I read you, Man. There is another alternative, but No, forget it."

"What, Man? What?"

"Well, there's this chick Monique visiting out here from the East Coast. I think she's from Montreal. Yeah, she's from Montreal or Quebec City, one of the two, and she's really into this revolutionary thing, you know what I mean? She's French Canadian, and she thinks she knows it all. She ain't too hip with us people out here."

"What'd you mean by ain't too hip?"

"Well, I mean, well, she is off into a head trip that West Coast folks don't read the newspaper about what's happening back East. We do, but we don't all share similar philosophies, Dig? She's a real piece of work, that's all. Will debate her agenda, point by point, with any and everybody. Even giving in to her argument doesn't seem to give her satisfaction. She will then go on to educate the person as to *why* knowing is important, even if they don't express any interest in continuing the conversation. Her jaw just keeps on flapping."

"Sounds like you've had personal experience with her," Paul commented politely. "Why did you mention her in the first place?"

"Well, she's got this van. She's out here for a while and she's driving by herself. I figured a healthy-bodied man could rap his way into her situation, you know, I mean she's a real looker, I mean an attractive woman. Definitely knows her shit, like real smart and such. So if you can get her past the political stuff, I imagine she would be good company." replied Kevin.

"I hear what you're saying," said Paul. "Just give me the way to hook up with her and see how it goes. Real conversation and wheels to get around the Island don't sound like a bad situation for a guy with no wheels and no friends around these parts. How do I go about meeting this lady?"

"The easiest way is to go out to Beacon Park at sunrise, that's in the downtown Victoria area. She is usually there from about six to around six thirty every morning meditating, journaling, and taking photos. Apparently, she is really into photography as well. I know the lady she's staying with and that's been her routine for the last several days. If you would just happen to be walking in the vicinity after she's done her meditation and strike up a conversation, with her mind all clear and fresh, she may be open to letting you travel with her."

Paul laughed and said, "I just might do that."

"There is one thing I think would be cool, if you agree," he said, shaking his red curly hair and stroking the beard on his freckled face. Kevin was average in height but had noticeably short legs. That, along with his beer belly, gave him the affable appearance of someone who was outgoing and easy to talk to. Paul immediately recognized why Kevin and DJ would be friends. "Even on the Island, your group from Oil Cans is well-known. We do a little music set in the evenings every now and then. We even got a wah wah pedal for your guitar sound. It would be Far Out if you joined us for our funk session tomorrow night."

"Thank you for the compliment, and if jamming with you and your friends goes toward repaying the hospitality, Cool!" Paul readily replied.

Kevin then got up and asked Paul to follow him. He led Paul downstairs to a room that was literally a shrine to the late great Johnny Allen Hendrix, otherwise known as Jimi Hendrix. Pictures of him performing on stages all over the world covered one wall. Even some pictures of him just hanging out as a regular guy were there to add another dimension to the tribute. A Fender Stratocaster guitar in one corner leaned against a life-sized poster of Hendrix. A signed album cover of *Are You Experienced* with the original psychedelic artwork dominated the impressive collection. Kevin even had the mug shot of Jimi's arrest photo taken the year before in Toronto. On May 3rd 1969, while checking his luggage at Toronto's Pearson Airport, Canadian customs had found a small amount of heroin and some hashish. Jimi was released on bail in time to perform at the Maple Leaf Gardens that night. He later appeared before a judge and was acquitted. Jimi claimed a fan had slipped the drugs into his bags without his knowledge. The judge was probably a fan himself, as all charges were dismissed and Jimi's future visitation to Canada was not affected.

Kevin handed Paul a sleeping bag and a book on meditation by a dude named Christmas Humphreys. "Here's some info that might improve your chances of hooking up with the lady. I'm sure you'll know how to work it into your rap." he laughed.

The next morning, after doing a bit of reading up on transcendental meditation, Paul went down to Beacon Hill Park. He saw what looked like the van Kevin had described, old and green. He knew she couldn't be too far away, so he walked a bit further. Ah, that must be Monique. 'Let's see if I remember this right.' He prepared himself. Then Paul went into a heavy dramatic act.

"A thousand pardons, Ma'am, but is this Beacon Hill?"

He knew not to interrupt a person deep into meditation but felt she wouldn't be put off by it. Paul thought Monique was probably skilled enough in the art that she couldn't be disturbed. And he was right. Monique didn't even look up as she remained in the state of consciousness she had achieved.

"Could this be? Are you partaking in that mystical, magical tour introduced by the Far East? Are you actually at this moment freeing yourself from all your fears and anxieties, achieving spiritual fulfillment?

"Yes, Yes. I can see this on your face. Allah Be Praised! This is incredible. Here it is at..." Paul checked his watch in a graceful gesture, "six twenty-five and I've just found one of those chosen few possessing Universal Wisdom - a wisdom found only by studying the teachings of the great sages who long ago discovered the secrets of Inner Happiness. Yes, yes. It is all very clear now. *Faith is the bird that fills the light and sings when the dawn is still dark.*"

He concluded his act in a theatrical playful style. He then strolled about ten yards to her left to read more of the book Kevin had given him.

Monique's face hadn't even changed expression. After a few minutes she took out a journal and pen and started to write. More minutes passed. Then Monique got up and began to walk towards her van, passing in front of Paul, still expressionless.

"Hello, Monique!"

Monique stopped and smiled. "Bonjour, Paul!"

Surprised, he asked, "Can everyone who meditates read minds?"

"Look, Monsieur. I am not interested in playing any of your little games. Kevin called and told Candice I would have a visitor named 'Paul' this morning. But when he called, he never stopped to think that I may have been sitting right next to her. You men are all alike, playing these silly games and expecting women to jump in line and follow as if we know nothing."

Paul instantly recalled Kevin's warning of trying not to go 'full on' with her in debate and decided to move in a different more friendly direction.

"Well," said Paul, "it's obvious you know more than the average woman, and it's obvious you know about my reason for being here at this godforsaken hour in the morning. Actually, I love this time of day. Quiet, restful, no crowds."

"Yes, a time when others are still preparing for the day to begin. And to you I will say you may share the expenses, providing you agree to keep your hands to yourself and not expect me to take care of you. So many men choose to burden women with menial chores and mothering as opposed to just accepting her as they would a male travelling partner."

"Entendu, Mademoiselle."

"Ah. Parlez-vous Francais?"

"No. Just saw this dude in a French flick rattle it off, thought it was cute. Though I have thought about taking a French speaking class and I may get around to doing that some day."

Monique laughed. "Yes, Yes, but of course. Would you like to join me for some tea or coffee? We need to talk further. I still reserve the right to change my decision to travel with you, if further conversation warrants it," said Monique in a very matter of fact way.

Paul said, "You sound like a Capricorn woman to me."

Monique said, "Why do you say that? I know so little of Astrology."

Paul wanted to say, 'If you had just finished living with an Astrology Freak, you'd have to believe there is some credibility to it.' But the source of his knowledge was not important.

"Capricorn women are earth sign folks. You know, straight up, direct," he explained. "I know a little bit about astrology, more than I wish I did, actually. I read somewhere that Capricorn women are also calculating and smooth manipulators."

Monique said, "You mean, after talking to me for five minutes, you have labeled me a manipulator?" Her eyes were wide with astonishment. "Is that correct?"

Quickly Paul softened. "They also detest criticism. But don't fret none. I know that once you cross a Capricorn, you can cross her off your list. We have a long trip ahead so I'll try my best to make it a pleasant one."

He was truly impressed with everything about Monique. Wavy dark brown hair framed a small fine-featured face with sensuous hazel eyes. She had a body to die for, petite and curvy, accentuated by jeans that hugged her hips and applauded her ample behind. Kevin was right; she was a looker.

Monique said, "Two things, Paul. First, I don't like being labeled; and second...*just be yourself!* It makes conversation so much easier when you know who you are talking to, not some make-believe character."

They found a little café just a half block from where Monique had parked. The conversation flowed so smoothly, it was as if they had known each other for years. Yet at the same time, Paul felt an undercurrent of growing excitement. After they'd finished their coffee and loosely discussed travel plans, Monique drove him back to Kevin's and said she would see him later. She'd heard he was a musician from Vancouver and would be joining Kevin's friends. She and her girlfriend planned to come to the jam session that evening.

That night, Paul found that playing his guitar with Monique in the room was the best way to introduce himself without a lot of unnecessary fanfare. His music was definitely a link to his true persona. He admired Hendrix but what sane human being could follow his path as a role model? He'd enjoyed the musicians' life he'd lived in Vancouver, but felt it was more of an out of body experience. The other musicians around him ate, lived and breathed for each and every performance. For him, it was more of a trip keeping up with their enthusiasm than riding the wave alongside them.

To his pleasure, after the jam Monique came up to him and greeted him warmly in a very familiar manner. She said, "Very nice Paul! But the person Monique is interested in is brave enough to leave his comfort zone to truly grow and move forward."

"I am ready, Miss Monique!" Paul answered with honest enthusiasm. 'I am so ready for this kind of woman, straight to the point and mature,' he thought to himself.

CHAPTER 19

THE NEXT MORNING THEY HEADED THE ONLY DIREC-
tion possible by land: *north*. A short distance from Victoria,
the highway started to climb and soon they were driving
over the Malahat Mountains looking down on the dark sparkling ocean.

Monique's voice broke the water's hypnotic hold. "Well,
let's get the number one question on my mind out of the way.
How do you justify your involvement in Vietnam? I mean, I
would give my life for the FLQ, but I would have great diffi-
culty taking someone else's life for the cause. And yet soldiers
are expected to take lives. Do you have any remorse?"

"Well first off, although I was trained to kill and mentally
prepared for it, fortunately I was assigned to the Medical
Unit and my job was to save lives. I was truly grateful for that
role. And I can say that I proudly served my country and supported my brother marines for doing what they had to do to
fulfill *their* role in combat."

Both Paul and Monique rode in silence for what seemed
to be a long time, thinking about a discovery of something
they had in common. *Commitment to a Cause, without moral com-
promise, and without causing mortal harm.*

The way she spoke was a little scary with her machine gun style of asking questions and her extreme directness. Paul could understand some people being put off by her straightforward way and consequently judging her negatively. But he liked it. He felt it added value to their conversation.

Monique broke the silence. "I drove as far West from my Eastern roots as I could go to try to find a positive environment away from all the constant chaos. There is a great deal of conflict happening right now in Québec, the rest of Canada and the world. On a personal level, I felt I was having *battle burnout* and losing my ability to be effective. The Temptations called it a Ball of Confusion."

Paul quickly answered, "Wow, when I spent several weeks in a hospital in 'Nam, that's the tune that kept running through my head. *A Ball of Confusion* is so fitting to describe the world today."

"I arranged through my university in Montréal to take a short sabbatical in exchange for providing a few seminars at the University of Victoria related to my studies in Political Science. Thought it would be a welcome break. Instead, I found people who were either uninformed or misinformed about what was going on in Québec. So many lacked common knowledge of my world. My hope is to someday be a Professor of PoliSci, or at least that is my goal at present.

"The last year of my studies was focused on the political writings of Niccolo Machiavelli. Are you aware of him, Paul?" She didn't wait for an answer. "Well, the crux of his philosophy is that 'anyone setting up a Republic and establishing a constitution for it should assume that all men are wicked and will always give vent to their evil impulses whenever they have the chance to do so.' My theory is that this is not necessarily true and I am creating an argument that will either prove or disprove Machiavelli's teachings using the French Canadian situation as the model.

"We are telling Canada to understand our vision of equality as fellow Canadians. Does this government ignore us based on their evil impulse to control, or is control just another form of greed and manipulation in general? A person without a vision will simply become a non-entity. It is important for people to feel good about the direction their lives are moving in. At this time we don't believe the majority of our countrymen understand that our future is one and the same."

Paul flinched. He could easily see the same argument could be made right now in the United States with the struggle for Black identity and acceptance. But for him, the mission was not about preaching Blackness. He was not raised to feel disenfranchised. He belonged to that tiny group of Black folks who were enjoying what America had to offer. That is until he went to Vietnam and lived with those who were not a part of the American Dream. Brothers dying for a country that did not recognize them as equal.

She continued, "So I found myself being asked to share my vision of The Québécois with different classrooms on campus in Victoria."

He politely nodded and listened to her every word. The similarity between her vision for *all* of Canada to show more respect for the French Canadian culture strongly aligned with what Sergeant Harris had been rapping about back in 'Nam and what was happening right now in the ghettos and Black communities all over America. *Was his being raised to think of himself as different from other Blacks the cause of his discontentment and the driving force to find his own identity?* He had come to think this was the case while convalescing after the head injury. There had been a lot of time for self-reflection.

Now the goal was to find his role, and becoming the next Hendrix wasn't it. Hendrix's style of celebrity was way too self-serving. Richie Havens, on the other hand, was a total class act and a role model in his own way. So it wasn't wrong to be Jimi, but it just wasn't for him. He definitely grooved on the style of Havens, but didn't like dealing with the public - and that came hand in glove with being famous.

They stopped for gas and takeout in Nanaimo then continued up island. Soon they passed an abandoned oyster packing plant surrounded by mountains of shells with mother of pearl catching the rays of the sunlight from a million different angles. Monique saw a photo op she couldn't resist.

She had seemingly thousands of dollars worth of camera gear. She used many different lenses - one for close shots, another for distant shots like the eagle they saw in a nest. She seemed to have everything she could possibly need to get the shot she wanted. She had already planned to get portraits of the Native Indian kids they were sure to see. The ones he had seen back in Vancouver had reminded him so much of the kids in the project housing back in the Tenderloin of San Francisco and he hoped the children on the Island would not have that same *startled urban look*. Regardless, whatever the photo opportunity, she had the equipment.

And so began Paul's introduction to photography. She was a patient and thorough instructor and Paul enjoyed playing the role of her assistant.

"Hand me that lens, Paul. Always use a wide angle lens for this kind of shot. Be aware of the sunlight and how it may affect your picture."

She was specific and direct in her manner in all things.

Their next stop was Rathtrevor Provincial Park, a huge natural bay looking out to several islands and mainland British Columbia in the distance. The tide was all the way out and the entire beach was dotted with hundreds of pure white sand-dollars. They stopped to eat the food they'd bought earlier and then walked, took photos, and just soaked in the perfection of the moment. Paul felt himself relaxing more than he had in a very long time. While watching the light fade on the water as the sun was setting behind them, they decided this was the perfect place to spend the night. Paul was aware of the sexual tension building between them but felt honor bound to stick to their *hands off* agreement since it was only their first night together.

Back in the van the next morning, they continued their trip through quaint, folksy Parksville then into Qualicum Beach, an obvious artists' colony which reminded him a lot of Sausalito. Everything seemed to have slowed down to a different vibe and he felt Monique was riding the same mellow wave. Every time they saw something worthy of a photo, they stopped and so the day drifted on. Though back on the beach they had shared some quality weed, being high without chemicals was truly a new experience.

They continued driving north past the Air Force Base at Comox then on up to Campbell River. It was here they again stopped for the night.

Paul really wanted to devour her, right then and there, but that was the old Paul. And this was Monique, not a groupie. Sure, it would be breaking one of her rules 'of keeping his hands to himself,' but he knew they were in a totally different space from when she'd given him that order. He wanted more than immediate gratification with Monique. He felt she wanted the same, but he wasn't completely certain. After all, this was only their second full day together. He looked for her permission, not wanting to force something that she may not be feeling yet to the same degree he was. He knew she would get there, so why rush things?

Dinner was quiet with fresh salmon, a good bottle of wine, and some great smoke. Then they drifted off to sleep in each other's arms. This was already a major improvement from the night before. Somewhere in the cobwebs of his mind, Nat King Cole was singing 'and too many moonlight kisses seem to fade with the morning sun.' Paul did not want that to be the case this time. He accepted her warmth and the close contact for just what it was. He imagined that *right now* was like enjoying the aroma and anticipation of a simmering stew. And inevitably, a delicious meal would follow.

The next morning they set off to Port Hardy at the northern tip of the Island.

As they drove by a group of young First Nations children playing, Monique just had to stop and photograph them. They spent the rest of the day interacting and photographing the charismatic kids and their elders who were sitting in the shade watching over them.

The children were so receptive. Monique high-fived and hugged the kids in such a natural, easy way as they posed and played with her. Their clothes were not new and some were too big, probably hand-me-downs from older brothers and sisters. But they were proud and happy kids, open to the little toys and gifts Monique had brought. She'd been advised by her girlfriend who'd visited this community previously that gifting would be appropriate...and received with gratitude.

That night during dinner Paul commented, "You truly seemed to enjoy interacting with those kids today. Have you ever thought about having children of your own?"

"I have a son, he is about the age of the children we photographed today," she answered quietly without hesitation.

Trying not to show his astonishment, Paul gently asked, "And where is he right now?"

"Before I answer, maybe I should tell you a bit more about myself." Monique took a deep breath and it was obvious to Paul that this was not easy for her to speak about. "I am the youngest of a family of fourteen, from a poor neighbourhood in Montréal. My mother's sister asked if she could raise me. She was wealthy through marriage to a rich Englishman and couldn't have children of her own. My mother was struggling to feed us all and knew the opportunities I would have, so she allowed my aunt and uncle to take me and raise me as their own child. I was given everything money could buy - the best of schools, trips abroad, anything and everything I wanted. I did not know they were not my real parents until one of my drunken uncles told me at a Christmas party who my true mother was. I became so angry.

"Pourquoi? Why? I really don't know why. But I felt the need to rebel. I somehow felt I was not deserving of my secure and bountiful upbringing. I felt I été dupé - was tricked"

Paul was stunned. 'Another life experience mirrored,' he thought. Now he could fully explain why he'd joined the Marines and she would understand. But he couldn't interrupt now, and so she continued.

"All my childhood, I had defended my privileged life to those I was raised to believe were my cousins. I had accepted the stories that they were poor and less educated because of their own laziness and lack of ambition when, in actuality, we were from the same gene pool. I started running around and rebelling and I found another rich kid to make mischief with a few doors down. We got pregnant. They married us at sixteen, the moment they discovered I was 'with child.' When his parents discovered I was planning to raise our child near Little Burgundy, they had the marriage annulled. Louis and I were only children ourselves and very weak.

"They took my baby, ended our marriage, and left me with nothing. My aunt and uncle did continue to support me at an expensive boarding school and I entered McGill at seventeen. I promised myself I would never again be as weak as I had been back then. My power would come from my education."

She took a deep breath and seemed to relax a little, almost as if the worst part was over.

"It was not very difficult for me to become emotionally involved with my peoples' struggle, my fellow Québécois. I received my degree in Political Science. Then I went on for my masters at McGill and will be completing my doctoral degree shortly. I hope to teach at one of the Montréal campuses. I'm on a self-ordained track to become the youngest and first female chair of the humanities department of the university, and here I am now."

Paul thought of an old Dean Martin song line, "well ain't that a kick in the head!"

He was speechless. What an awesome story, what an awesome person.

CHAPTER 20

AFTER BREAKFAST THE NEXT MORNING, THEIR journey took them back down the same highway. The Island was predominantly a forest sparsely populated in small pockets of communities here and there, mostly along its coastlines. They passed by spots they had previously visited, but now Monique seemed to be in driving mode and not into stopping. She seemed deep in her own thoughts and Paul gave her space. They were heading south to a place called Coombes where an old-fashioned general store apparently had goats grazing on its grass roof.

"Goats have always tripped me out," Paul calmly broke the quiet. "They have such interesting expressions on their faces and in their eyes. No wonder they are so often tied to mystical and metaphysical folklore. Look at that one to the left, Wow!"

"I feel the same as you, Mon Ami," Monique answered. "They are such interesting creatures." They'd been driving for several hours so when they reached the general store they had stopped to grab some food. They continued to enjoy their comfortable silence while exploring the store that seemed to have everything, *including* the kitchen sink!

Paul tried to sneak glances at Monique when she was not watching. She was wearing a cotton blouse that tied in the front. Her breasts were a little larger than the loose shirt showed, but she was neither showcasing nor underplaying them. That really turned him on. His dreamed of 'Banquet of Lovemaking' was ready to boil over, and he was more than ready to explore every inch of her.

Getting back in the van, they headed west past Port Alberni through Cathedral Park Grove where giant Douglas Firs reminded him of Big Sur and California's Redwoods. They followed the winding, former logging road out to the coast to the tiny community of Tofino kneeling on Long Beach. The wild natural beach with seals and huge crashing waves definitely reminded him of home. Not surprising. It was still the open coastline of the Pacific Ocean, as it was in California, only much further north.

On the drive out he shared with her more of his war experience. Again, she asked him if he had believed in what he was doing as a Marine. What was his interpretation of the slavery experience? She readily agreed that the French had not arrived in North America the way his ancestors had arrived. But the mentality of the colonized in *The Wretched of the Earth* was a *mutual entity* and just as despicable as Frantz Fanon had exposed in his final publication.

Her questions forced him to think and clarify issues he had up until now avoided. He answered them as he had answered her before with complete honesty and no pretention. He spoke from an open heart and hoped her heart was opening to him as well.

Then her questions became a little more personal when she looked him straight in the eyes and asked: "Can you define the word Love?" Paul pondered deeply. He'd never been asked that question before.

Then Monique replied, not waiting for his response: "Only a fool would try to generically define something which is so personal an experience. To some it means unconditional security and support throughout their lives. To others, it is a feeling of complete surrender and submission to another person or, for that matter, an ideology. I can only say this: after all that has come between me and the father of my child I still feel something very special for him. I used to blame him for just giving into the whole mess, but then I realized neither of us could have changed anything. I still love him and I will always love the child that we brought into this world. For me, *this is love*. I kept the first blanket my son was wrapped in after he was born. It goes with me no matter where I travel. I can still remember how he smelled and how he felt in my arms, whatever the time or wherever the place. I am emotionally tied to him for always."

Paul said, "You can't imagine how beautiful our time together is to me. I've been running around like a maniac, worrying about who I am. Where was I going? Just running scared I guess. Then I met this guy, and he said, Live for Love. Of all things, this guy was a gigolo. I ignored his words purely because I was raised to disrespect people who live as parasites.

"But Wow, *Live for Love* - the way those words bothered me. Because I took what he was saying literally. I was raised to be the Man, the person in charge. The one whose responsibility it is to make things happen. You don't just live for whatever may come along and that includes this thing called Love! How could this dude tell me how to live when he didn't follow his own words? His entire life focused on what he could GET from someone. But where was *the quality*? The *something* beyond just entering another person's body... or purse for that matter?

"I found myself questioning and listening deeper to what was happening around me and trying to get more out my existence. I focused on the music I was playing, the lady I was living with, the people I was hanging with. And the more I questioned, the more I realized I was not where I wanted to be. I'm listening better since I made the decision to leave my so-called comfortable surroundings and I'm feeling good, very good about where I'm at today. I'm on solid ground for what might be the very first time. Wherever that takes me, I'm ready for it."

That evening, they checked into a nice little Motor Lodge with a restaurant. The tables had red checkered cloths and Chianti wine bottles with candles sprouting from their necks. Paul and Monique enjoyed a simple spaghetti dinner in this charming place. While they were finishing the last of the wine,

Paul said, "These last two days, being with you, I have really allowed myself to let go a bit. *Thank you*, Monique." They returned to their room with expectations of ravishing each others' bodies, each knowing that nothing would be held back.

As the door to the room locked behind them, Paul reached over and touched her hand. He then shifted and pressed his lips to Monique's. She allowed the tip of his tongue to feel every bit of her full mouth while hers did the same. He felt her meeting his energy. They were playful at first, and then gave into pure physical enjoyment as their kisses deepened. They let their tongues be the introduction by pressing and caressing, searching for more, feeling more passion than he'd ever imagined. Time and space had lost all meaning. It was only them, lost in each other. Placing his hands on her shoulders, he experienced a thrill like never before as she allowed herself to be enveloped by his full frame, her body pressed against his. He felt the beating of her heart, the smell of her moist skin, the warmth of a woman seeking a union she desired completely. Every point of touch, every sensation was exquisitely isolated... then melded together.

The message was clear as he softly whispered into her ear, "I want you as much as I am feeling you want me. We can make this thing work. I want more than today. I want as much of you as you are willing to give."

She responded, "Let's let our lovemaking decide what tomorrow will bring!"

There in that tiny room with jasmine incense burning and candles flickering shadows on the walls, they kissed and touched and loved. The power to feel more and more of one another was boundless. Minnie Ripperton called it *riding inside my love*. He felt her body tremor when he entered her. Being inside her, he seemed to feel everything with heightened awareness. Initially he'd thought he was about to crush her small frame beneath him, but she locked her arms tighter as if saying "Bring it on, Big Guy. I can match whatever you got to give."

And they loved on and on into the night.

CHAPTER 21

WHEN THEY RETURNED TO VICTORIA, PAUL AND Monique moved into a room at her friend's house. Candice was visiting friends in Vancouver so they had the place to themselves. Living with Monique was an entirely different experience from living with Jennifer. Both were very attractive, so obvious admiration and come-ons from guys were commonplace. But whereas Jennifer had usually drawn attention to the flirtations or made a scene, Monique either ignored them or simply smiled graciously.

Somehow Paul felt inconspicuous when he was with Monique. Well, truthfully he would stand out in any crowd. Being six foot four made him too big to hide and his Louisiana red-toned chocolate complexion made him too dark to blend with the predominately white faces around them. But somehow he didn't feel on display with Monique; they were simply two people out and about. This comfort level was brand new. The people around him hadn't changed, so obviously it was a mindset shift on his part. But how? And why? Yeah, Monique really made him feel they were the only people around.

Monique's notoriety had escalated with the news of increased terrorist activity in Quebec. But her brilliant style of fielding questions and educating with further questions rather than defending some outrageous act, made her more like a news reporter or a celebrity guest with additional knowledge. In this way, she avoided being judged as a participant. She had a couple more speaking engagements around the campus, but they shared the rest of their time with each other.

One night as they drove to dinner, Paul said, "You know there is a street in San Francisco called Grant Avenue that has a red gateway arch with Chinese characters and symbols almost exactly like this one. I ate at a Chinese restaurant the first night I was in Victoria with Kevin and found out that Victoria has the second largest population of Chinese on the West Coast next to San Francisco. The chef was cruising through the restaurant and I asked him why their food tasted somewhat different than what I was used to back home. You know what he told me? Here they are able to import spices directly from Hong Kong that couldn't be imported into the States."

Monique added, "In Montréal there is a large group of Asians as well, but nowhere near the size of the Asian population here in Victoria."

Her comment answered another question he had wondered about — ethnic diversity in Montreal.

At this point in his life, he had come to realize that wherever the road took him, *the human experience was the same*. No matter the color of their skin or what language they spoke, for everyone life's struggles are all similiar. Being around and living comfortably with different ethnicities *had to happen*. In spite of governments controlling whatever they could, it was all about sharing and savoring the diversities as well as the commonalities.

Paul and Monique enjoyed many different ethnic restaurants around Victoria. "It seems the universal talent of students is knowing where to find the tastiest and cheapest food," Monique noted.

Victoria was the capital of British Columbia, but was quite a bit smaller and quieter than Vancouver. This made it a desirable retirement location. But at this time of year, the town was overrun with tourists. Its beauty and old world charm made it a popular vacation destination. All in all, it was very different territory for both of them and they enjoyed exploring it together.

Everyday ordinary tasks felt like an event when they were together. When he wasn't with Monique, Paul spent his time enjoying his new second favorite form of entertainment: developing the rolls and rolls of film they had taken on their travels. The university had a photo lab that Monique had full access to and she got permission for Paul to use it too. What a thrill watching images materialize...images that had become memories now reappearing. Photography would be something that he would enjoy for the rest of his life. Another gift from Monique.

The library was another place Monique reintroduced to Paul. Following her meditation sessions, she often visited the library to research or find information to add to different projects she was working on. Paul easily adapted to her routines. The smell of the books coupled with the feeling he experienced when seeking new knowledge all came back to him. As a child, he remembered spending hours at a time exploring the Bible as well as The *Encyclopedia Britannica* and *Poor Richard's Almanack* in their library at home. The university had a multiethnic section that included books like *The Autobiography of Malcolm X*; books by Frantz Fanon and Albert Memmi and even Ralph Ellison's *The Invisible Man* had taken on a deeper meaning since he'd initially read it in his freshman English class at Stanford. Paul had continued reading these authors while in Vietnam along with other books Sergeant Harris had turned him on to.

Monique and he hooked up with several students who were adventurers like themselves around 'U Vic.' They shared photographs and memories of Vancouver Island with each other, appreciating what a special little pocket of the planet they'd discovered.

One morning when Monique walked out of the shower, Paul was at the little table in the corner of the living room. The big bay window had become their favorite spot on lazy mornings like this one. It overlooked the spot where the edge of the campus merged with Victoria's residential streets.

Monique threw on an oversized Université à Montréal tee-shirt over her panties and joined him with a cup of coffee.

"You got up pretty early, Monsieur and you're looking like you're a million miles away," she said quietly as she propped her feet up on the seat of the chair and took another sip of the warm brew.

"You know, we've talked about politics, but never in any great detail." Paul continued, "I guess what I'm saying is, Monique, you've never once filled me in on the FLQ Movement specifically."

Monique said, "Oui, and you've never spoken of your Peoples' struggle. Yes, bits and pieces, but just like you, I want to know more. I have forever been an admirer of Martin Luther King, Jr. A person willing to stand up to every possible evil with his vision of a better world, for not only his people but for all mankind, is beyond magnifique."

Paul said, "Well, first of all, I too wholeheartedly believe in Dr. King's teachings. His assassination affected me to the core. And we will talk more about him later. But for now, what does FLQ mean? What do the letters stand for again?"

Monique said, "Front de Libération du Québec which translates to the Liberation Front of Quebec."

Paul asked, "And what is your main objective?"

"We want to answer the challenge of the status quo, the existing state of affairs. We want to answer the challenge of the business men who believe they can maintain the current political and economic system by sowing *fear of change* among the population. We do not believe we, the French Canadians, are getting our fair share of the overall power in Canadian society."

Paul asked, "And how does your group answer the challenge?"

"To the threats of the royal trust we offer real bombs. All we are doing is answering their violence with counter-violence. We are defending ourselves against the constant attacks of the anti-worker, anti-Québec forces that make up the Financial Institutions, the Big Corporations, the Chamber of Commerce and so on. Then there is another group who call themselves the Liberal Party, but many of my people don't feel that they are fighting for the good of all. No, they're just primarily fighting for themselves, making themselves more rich."

Paul thought back to his father saying on several occasions how important it was to be on the inside of business deals and it was who you knew that helped you get ahead in this world. He'd never before thought of it as taking away from those in need but rather as benefits for those able to use them. *Time to rethink that.*

Monique continued, "We are fighting this very minute against the owners of the communication conglomerates who continue to spew out the **lie** that the current government serves all of society. It is clear the current government serves only those who finance it. They are not supporting democracy, as Salon intended. They want eternal servitude. You place that in context with Machiavelli's conclusion that 'all men are basically evil' and it sets up the justification of a Stalin, Hitler, and every other megalomaniac who uses whatever rhetoric necessary to make people blindly obey their self-adulatory wishes. Here in North America we will call it capitalism."

Without stopping the conversation, Monique padded into the bedroom and grabbed a pair of jeans. She returned to the table and pulled them on before sitting back down. In what could only be described as a quieter version of a *rally cry* she continued: "We are fighting these Capitalist pigs who monopolize all the major means of information dispersal and who are trying to make it seem that *we* are the enemy of the People of Québec. Not the so-called 'Liberal' Party, lead by Pierre Trudeau. We all fought so hard for him to become the Prime Minister...Trudeaumania we called it. There is now some speculation that he will turn against the very people who ensured his election victory. He is threatening to invoke the War Measures Act, giving the government power to arrest without trial anyone perceived to be a terrorist.

"There are many excellent minds in Québec who believe Québec is strong enough socially and powerful enough economically to separate from Canada. I have not totally sided with them, but I do not believe that they should be treated as terrorists and enemies of the state simply because the civil rights of their people need to be improved. And most importantly, not all Québécois are terrorists."

Paul interrupted, "J. Edgar Hoover says Blacks are the enemy and must be contained and destroyed when necessary. Not all Blacks are members of The Black Panthers, but Hoover tries to make America believe that they are one and the same."

Monique got up and stretched her arms overhead. As she ran her hands through her long dark hair she said, "We just held an International Conference in Montréal on Black Power. It was put together primarily by the West Indian brothers at Sir George Williams College and Stokely Carmichael and several Caribbean activists were invited to speak. Their courage and struggles have mirrored many of our struggles. Unfortunately, egos from both sides could not see enough similarities to work together, and overall the conference failed, in my opinion.

"There was one positive though. The message *Blackness is a State of Mind* was heard loud and clear. It's not the color of your skin or whether you are listed as French Canadian; it's a state of mind. How you see yourself determines your pride in being Black or a proud French Canadian."

Paul said, "I'm sure you are familiar with Albert Memmi's *The Colonizer and the Colonized?*" Monique's talk had again triggered a recollection of previous knowledge he had forgotten.

Monique replied, "Certainement Monsieur."

Paul pulled out a copy of the book from his backpack that was sitting on the floor beside him and continued, "Well, in his preface he raps about how the idea for the book came about and how he felt he knew what the Algerians, Moroccans, and all my African brothers would get out of his book. And he even felt North Americans and South Americans could gain insight from it."

"Mais Oui! His book was published in 1957, a little while after our struggle had been rekindled," said Monique. She continued, "Historically, Paul, the war began in 1759, after the British took over Lower Canada at the Plains of Abraham. As far as this generation is concerned, it was brought back to a subtle yet lucid awakening just a few years ago, when we became a political force by taking half the popular vote in the Federal Election in '68 making Pierre Trudeau, Prime Minister."

Just then, loud honking from the street below seemed to punctuate her last statement. They both laughed.

Paul continued to ask his questions. "How many French Canadians are there?"

Monique answered, "I really can't say; this is a question that Census Canada could answer, you would think, but statistics can be manipulated in any manner the government chooses.

"You'd be surprised Paul, but it's not only French Canadians who believe that Canada should be recognized as bilingual with both French and English as our official languages. Nor do all believe that our system of government works for all Canadians equally. We have support outside of Québec as well."

Paul nodded. "You are a Political Scientist, first and foremost, and you see everything from that point of view. Laws governing society whether just or unjust, are made by politicians. Who for the most part are looking out for themselves. The U.S. remains divided on many levels, as well. For example, in certain states it is still illegal for Blacks and Whites or Asians and Whites to be married. *Right now! In 1970!* How can a law dictate who can share love, who can marry, or who can raise children together?"

"Precisely," agreed Monique. "But is it really about love? The kind we are sharing right now, you and I? For the politicians it's about two things only: Greed and Power. More about **Greed** actually, using whatever means necessary to acquire more than their share, from the warring chieftains of early societies to the thieves in our own time. We are in solidarity with all struggles waged by people who are victims of North American Imperialism. We support the struggle led by those first exploited on this continent, the Indians otherwise known as First Nations Ancestors. We are in solidarity with your people in America and Cuba who are also fighting Yankee Imperialism."

Paul answered, "Yeah, but your people don't wear a twenty-four hour uniform that is the color of their skin. You would think that people of color would have a natural reason to come together, but it doesn't happen."

Monique replied, "But as I said before, it's the *State of Mind*. You know how important this is, Oui? You shared with me your discussions with Harris while in Vietnam. You mentioned your understanding of the colonized mentality. Then why would it be so difficult for you to understand the confusion?"

Paul said, "I hear ya, Babe. I think that's the trouble with a lot of my people. They think that just because they're born with a darker hue, that Black Consciousness and awareness of all People of Color is automatic. It took me almost dying in a Vietnam jungle and meeting fellow Brothers trapped in their world without education or any idea that life can be different than what it is today. But I was blessed, I was more fortunate; therefore, I owe it to myself to give back, help others and show there can be better. I am finding it hard to feel truly *free* while others are still suffering in so many ways."

Monique said, "True, our struggles are different, yet the same. I also was told to forget my cultural roots and become one with *them*, the establishment. They give us token advancement, which comforts a few, then take our most able leaders and brainwash them into becoming the colonizers. Then one day those *would be leaders* realize they were only tools used to hold anyone not on their team, down."

"Yeah. We were born a thousand miles apart, but listening to you, along with some of my recent reads, this may sound a little over the top, I mean too melodramatic, but I came across this in *The Prophet* while reading it this morning:

> *I suffered at the hands of despotic rulers;*
>
> *I suffered slavery under insane invaders;*
>
> *I suffered hunger imposed by tyranny;*
>
> *Yet, I still possess some inner power*

With which I struggle to greet each day.

Paul felt himself drifting off mentally, so he changed the topic. "You know we've been together for about three weeks now and I just can't get over how poised and collected you stay. When you rap about the FLQ you sound more like a commissioned officer. Tell me, how deep is your involvement?" Paul asked.

"I know many serious FLQ Members who are growing very impatient with how slowly things are changing. They are very scary, Mon Cher. I fear that sometime soon, someone will die. But right now, today, it is mostly the students who are making their voices heard. And I have chosen to continue to educate and enlighten the *youth* of today. *We will change this world.*

"As a Professor, I will open the minds of many more until *the World* will truly become *right*; not just for some, but for *All*"

Then she whispered, "If only you would come home with me, I could really show you what I talk about and share back at the university. Then you could see Montréal as I know it. Come visit *My World*...won't you come with me?"

Paul said, "Well, I don't know. Not right now... maybe in a few months or so."

He was surprised by his reluctance to go to Montreal with Monique. He was doing jack shit with his life; he hadn't a clue, and this woman seemed to be the exact opposite of him. Monique was focused, determined, and driven. Then it hit him. It wasn't about traveling to the East Coast. It was about his surging feelings and his unexpected attachment to her. He kept following those wonderful dark eyes as she talked with wonderment and pride. She was *Magnifique.*

In the midst of listening to Monique, listening to the voice within his mind, and trying to make some sense out of the moment at hand, a song by the Beatles featured on their 1969 album *Abbey Road* came on. Was it on the radio? Was it being played from nearby? Paul did not know, but the moment was magical.

He began looking at Monique with eyes he'd been afraid to *use*. The lyrics had been heard a hundred times before. "Something in the way she moves attracts me like no other lover." Monique just had it! What IT was did not matter. She had IT and everything about her just felt so good. He continued to intertwine the lyrics with her persona and felt every nerve ending begin to tingle.

Completely oblivious to Paul's feelings, Monique said, "I am not trying to recruit you to join our struggle. I'm not trying to sell you on the validity of our fight. I really feel you would enjoy Montréal." She was silent for a moment, then said, "I'm trying to say that the past few weeks have been perfect for me, and I hope you feel the same."

"Monique, wait. I think you're missing something here. The past couple of weeks with you have been *more than beautiful for me*, spiritually as well as mentally. There hasn't been a person that I have wanted to be with and who I could honestly relate to for quite some time now, maybe even never before. I just don't want to hurt you or even get hurt myself, by not being able to give you all of me, everything you deserve," said Paul.

He began to hear himself, how ridiculous he sounded. So contradictory. In one breath, he was telling this woman how fantastic she was, and at the same time, something about deserving!?

She had attracted him like no one else...period! Nothing else mattered. This feeling, this present situation, had to be embraced and explored completely. And he was ready for whatever that would be. And it felt good. Be it *love and happiness* or to discover it was *not to be forever*, who knows? But they had to find out.

Monique said, "Paul, you always seem to make things more difficult than they really are. If you are afraid to use the word *love*, then don't. But understand that true friendship means just that. We are true friends, and I feel that Montréal would be good for you. Nothing more. Nothing less."

Paul said, "Yeah, you're right. Monique, I would very much like to go home with you. True and real connections are hard to find. But how did you know I was deserving of your love? What was it about me that attracted you?"

"You remind me of myself. Your search for real love was my search as well. A love where each could grow and transform with the security and support of knowing their love would be safe, a love built on a foundation *of mutual respect and admiration,* and of course, *Grande Passion*. I felt this almost from the moment I first saw you, and our lovemaking confirmed it."

CHAPTER 22

AFTER A LONG SLOW TRIP ACROSS CANADA, THEY arrived in Montreal just after daybreak. Monique had driven through the stunningly clean streets of Montréal, passing the campuses of the University of Quebec and then McGill University. Paul liked McGill instantly - the open gate, the ivy-covered red brick walls, a plaque declaring its charter granted in 1821.

Monique had slowed down and pointed to a building. "That is the Redpath Museum; my office and the Political Science faculty is just around the corner. The downtown campus is spread over eighty acres with more than one hundred buildings," she said proudly.

'It's a strong visual of a Mecca of Knowledge and Learning,' Paul thought to himself.

She then turned onto a street called Côte Des Neiges past the McGill General Hospital and drove to Mont-Royal Park. Paul felt the crisp morning air caress him as they climbed out of the van and stretched. He then followed Monique up a mountain path away from the parking area to a lookout over the city.

Monique said, "We are looking at the Saint Lawrence River. Montréal is an island. There to the east is Old Montréal and east again of that bridge, the Jacque Coterie Bridge. Over there, the area known as Little Burgundy is where most of the Black families live; a little further over is the Irish community. We pride ourselves here in Montréal in not having what your cities call slums.

"Montréal's industry consisted primarily of large factories until the Seaway industry opened up different jobs and opportunities. And of course there was always the train industry. Many Blacks worked as porters and such. In front of us is the Sunlight Building. That bridge over there," she pointed, "is the Victoria Bridge. And next to it is 'Fat Town,' otherwise known as Westmount, the upper class English district. To the north is Outremont, where I grew up. Did you know that after New York, Montreal has the highest number of restaurants in North America?"

She stopped her sightseeing tour, kissed Paul, and said, "Enough of this idle chatter. If it takes me twenty years to show you my home, I will find more and more and then some more for you to love and enjoy." They then found a private spot and made love right there on the hill overlooking the city. While traveling across Canada, they had found many opportunities for spontaneous lovemaking. It was a habit they'd started *in their beginning* on Vancouver Island. It was a new experience for both of them to feel so free and uninhibited while still maintaining proper discretion, of course.

Monique lived in a little apartment not far from McGill, just off Peel Street. Concrete block bookshelves held what looked like a thousand books. Books were piled and scattered everywhere your eyes could travel. There were a few photographs with varying themes and some borrowed or found-at-curbside furniture. Overall, the look was 'sparse and books!' Obviously her focus was her studies, not entertaining as Jennifer's had been. Such opposites.

"I spend a lot of time in my books," Monique offered, "but I love my bed the most and have a feeling you will enjoy it as well. It seems no matter what kind of day I have endured, I know if I make it up those stairs and open my apartment door, my bed will be there waiting for me. My bedroom is my sanctuary, my place for renewal."

The bedroom was a stark contrast to the rest of the utilitarian apartment. Although very small, the ceiling was high and a sparkling chandelier hung from an ornate carved centerpiece. 'Wonderful to gaze at while lying in bed after some loving,' Paul thought to himself. The high, ornate brass bed sat at an angle and took up the entire room. It was covered with a quilt made from a multitude of small squares of velvet in dark jewel tones. Many lacy pillows were propped at the headboard along with some small beaded ones. Sheer purple curtains covered the tall narrow window. A tiny carved antique table was next to the bed and on it, a Tiffany Lamp draped with a deep red, fringed scarf. Paul would later discover that she kept her clothes in a wardrobe in the hall. And all those pillows, moved to the floor when they slept, were a challenge to navigate when getting up to the bathroom in the middle of the night.

Paul was unsure of the extent of Monique's political activities. At one point he thought they might be throwing bombs or robbing banks for the cause. It was a relief for him to discover that Monique was not a primary or even principal member of the FLQ. She was very much respected but more like Engels was to Marx. She was an intellectual supporter, not involved with bombs and mayhem. She was a trusted confidante to the serious players in the organization. In fact, as Monique shared with Paul, many of the FLQ leaders went out of their way to protect her from being recognized as a 'getting down and dirty' Revolutionist.

One night, as they were lying on the *Big Brass Bed*, which was really the only comfortable place to relax in the apartment, Paul sighed and said, "We seem to communicate so well with each other. We've been blessed starting our relationship as we did, out West in BC. Getting to know each other without *life's interferences and complications*. And as close as I feel to you right now, I feel there's so much more to uncover, to explore and develop between us. I mean, I feel so connected but most exciting to me is how we are laying groundwork for our future. I truly enjoy your company, your mind, and your body, and wow what a gorgeous body!!!"

Monique seemed to turn red all over and pressed herself into him. "Je suis d'accord...I agree," she whispered as she continued the intimacy. "Mon Cher, what I'm hearing is we've both experienced past relationships and know how easy it is to give up when things start becoming more difficult. Like my work. Soon, in just a few weeks, I will become extremely busy with my obligations to the outside world. I so hope that we have created a bond that will not allow anything to interfere with this world of *you and I*. You must know, I am as much in love with you as I was from the first time the dream became real. And there will come a time again when my work will not be in the way, I promise you. But yes, you must be prepared to share me with my other world. This will likely be difficult at times, but...how can I express it?...*doable!*"

"Until that time," Paul said, "We have to remember Vancouver Island, where we each found our soul mate. We have to make sure that magic carpet ride will continue. The outside world was *on hold*. But now we have to incorporate our other worlds into our love. That's cool. I can dig it. I think maybe I'm going to look around for a music gig or I'll just have too much time on my hands thinking about you getting back here and me *running inside your love!*" Paul could feel the grin he knew was on his face.

Monique paused for a moment to absorb his words and then smiled with a grin to match his. She'd heard the part about finding a job and felt it was a very sweet gesture. It told her he was willing to make an honest effort to keep the fire alive while sharing the living expenses.

"Two hearts on fire, feeding off one another, can melt away any and all obstacles! We *can* keep it going. Let us not worry about what tomorrow will bring. Come Paul, let us fortify our foundation with more lovemaking!"

And again they began their enjoyment of each other fully and absolutely.

A month passed like time was standing still, slow and easy. Then Monique began revving up for the coming semester. Paul would usually accompany her to the campus and find a suitable place to wait. He enjoyed sitting outside, either next to, or on the campus greens, reading or thinking. The time quietly became filled with '*What next?* This feels cool, but what kinda gig is out there waitin' to happen for me?'

One afternoon, Monique said with unexpected enthusiasm, "Hey, let's have some fun!"

"What'd ya have in mind?" Paul replied with interest.

"An old friend of mine just got back from Paris and there's a get together to welcome him back and find out what he's learned about current French politics. They will probably also speak about a program that turned out to be an amazing gathering of knowledge and brainpower, The Congress of Black Writers. I've mentioned it before. The one organized by West Indian students at McGill and Sir George Williams Universities and leaders of the city's Black community. Where Stokely Carmichael was amazing when he focused on using past atrocities as a unifying tool on the premise that *culture* is a cohesive force for people."

Paul was clueless about French politics, but he did know about Stokely. He knew he had left the Student Nonviolent Coordination Committee and was the 'Honorary Prime Minister' of the Black Panther Party and was also 'heir apparent' to Malcolm X who had been assassinated in 1965.

"Also," Monique continued, "a close friend of Frantz Fanon will surely be there. When Fanon died of cancer in 1961, Rene, who is also a psychiatrist, became the self-appointed, current world authority on Fanon and his teachings."

"Hey, I'm up for it," Paul responded, definitely intrigued. Besides, he couldn't resist the opportunity to see another piece of Monique's life away from their personal sanctuary.

That night Paul found himself walking into a section of Montreal he had only heard about in passing conversations: Outremont. The apartment building was just below the Mont Royale Lookout. Though he had never been to Europe, from all the foreign films he'd enjoyed, he imagined that this is what a high class, swanky neighborhood in Paris would look like. The streets were actually red bricks, not cobblestones, just like the streets of Old Montreal. Not in British Columbia or even San Francisco was there any architecture that compared to this. Then again, ancient history in San Francisco usually meant the Gold Rush era around 1849, while here in

Montreal the buildings dated back to the 1600s. Gas street lamps added to the quaint surroundings.

The doorman gave the first *eye-opener* of the evening when he greeted Monique as if she actually lived in the building. "Oh, so nice to see you again Mademoiselle!"

Next, when they walked into the apartment, *eye-opener* number two: an almost life sized photograph of Monique standing at a podium with a microphone in her hand. She had a look of intensity on her face Paul had never seen before, exuding radiance from a fierce fire within. The photograph, he had to admit, was a truly professional piece, capturing a spirit rarely caught as clearly, in a millisecond, as this shot had.

Life with Jennifer had seasoned Paul to the reality that there was past history in all relationships and there was no need to confess every detail of previous ones, as so many men made the mistake of doing. This photo, along with the doorman's greeting, screamed that Monique and this *old friend* had once had an intimate relationship. Every wall of the apartment featured pictures of easily recognizable world leaders or pictures one would see in *Life* or *National Geographic* magazines. It was obvious who had influenced Monique's interest in photography.

Before they had left their apartment, Monique had broken down a little back history on this friend. Jean Claude Belvoir was from Martinique. He had been raised in an upper middle class family and had attended the most prestigious high school in Martinique, the *Lycée* Schoelcher. Frantz Fanon had attended the same school. His father, a successful banker, had moved the family to Montreal after being recruited by the Bank of Canada for a leadership position.

Jean Claude had graduated from McGill with a Master's degree in Journalism. After graduation, with a little help from his father, the *Montreal Gazette* had hired him as a photojournalist. He'd married a French Creole woman of like socioeconomic status. Their four children attended the elite Catholic school of Saint Michel the Archangel. His job allowed him access to the world as an acclaimed photographer. At the age of 42, he seemed to have it all...all the world offered, yet, he felt something was missing. Monique volunteered more: "It is very common, here in Montréal, for men of his stature to have a mistress."

"So this is Paul," Jean Claude stated with an extremely warm, sincere smile and a strong handshake. He was a very handsome man who stood about six feet one or so with a caramel complexion. Jean Claude turned to encircle Monique in his arms but she stiffened and stepped back, placing her elbow between them and an outstretched palm against his chest.

"I'm here to introduce you to Paul and to hopefully enjoy interesting and stimulating conversation this evening," she stated, a little more formally than usual.

Paul found himself impressed with her response and felt that all his unwarranted fears of another man's involvement with *his woman* were senseless. Jealousy was not his thing and so the surge of possessiveness in response to the *eye-openers* had been unexpected. It had surprised him.

The most interesting person at the party turned out to be another Martinique transplant named Rene Le Claire, the friend of Fanon. He sat swirling a snifter of French brandy and said without being prompted, "Black Consciousness is imminent in its own eyes. But it was Frantz who pointed out the new horizons of possibility for French Québecers who had already begun to discern the need to remove themselves from the harsh conditions of colonial domination and to stop donning English masks. Stop speaking white. It was Fanon probing the psychosocial depths of anxiety and the mental violence of colonization."

He stopped talking long enough to empty and refresh his pipe, stoke it, and blow out a fragrant cloud of peach-scented tobacco. Then he continued, "The African American struggle and particularly the Black Power movement has caught the attention of people all over the world. This movement is characterized by remarkable *acts of bravery*. Black women and men put their lives on the line in the Southern States, peacefully demonstrating for their right to exist as free human beings... sheer bravery. Yet their courageous allies, White students and citizens, cannot be ignored. For they too are being brutalized by police, attack dogs and angry mobs.

"This was a scene that was acted out on French Canadian students as well. Last year, when I participated in the Black Congress affair across town, I must admit that the way Montreal Police and the Québec Government persecuted and prosecuted those students left no doubt that the hatred seen in the South was here in Montréal also.

"Remember Carmichael's response to someone in the audience asking him, 'How does one obtain the power to change something that is so steadfast in the World?' And he responded, 'I don't think that White Canadians would say that they stole Canada from the Indians.' Remember how everyone laughed. 'They said they took it ...and they did.' We all applauded. 'Well then, it's clear that we can't negotiate for these lands, we can't beg foe 'em, so we must take them. It's clear that we must take them through revolutionary violence.'

"It was obvious to me he was toying with the audience; the Brother was working the political climate of our time. But aside from that, the Organizers wanting to exclude all Whites was clearly untenable. The fact that they eventually decided to include the Whites revealed how fragmented the movement of developing a *Black Nation* really was!" added Dr. Le Claire, as he relived the moment.

Monique spoke without reservation, "I completely agree. And Jean Claude was in agreement with all Whites being excluded. *The Hypocrisy!*"

Jean Claude then jumped in on the talk, "Monique, we have discussed this before. I apologized for supporting White exclusion. It just slipped my mind that you were included as White." Everyone laughed except Monique. "I only meant that you are to me a child of the universe, not belonging to a specific race."

"Well, my friend, maybe that's why you've not seen my *universal* ass since. You knew my argument with the hardcore FLQ was that **All** those affected by Oppressors should stand together. I still love you as a brother, but that's as far as it goes after the way you disrespected me as you did on that day."

Eye-opener number three: the woman does not play games. She was open and very cordial the rest of the evening. Jean Claude had obviously got the message that Monique was not there to rekindle something, and quite frankly, the Brother didn't seem to be hurting. There were several young ladies and a couple of well-to-do older women who appeared to be vying to be the one to continue enjoying the evening at Jean Claude's after the gathering was over.

On the way home, Paul waited for Monique to discuss the night's proceedings, but she did not broach the subject. So Paul said nothing. He left it up to her to bring up the topic when she was ready.

The following morning, at the little table in the kitchen, Monique opened the conversation. "Why haven't you asked more about Jean Claude? Is it that you do not care to know, or are you afraid of what you may hear?"

Paul wanted to come up with something clever like Rhett Butler's "Personally, I just don't give a damn." But he knew that was untrue and that it would maybe even be an unrecoverable mistake to joke around, considering the tone of her voice.

"No Monique, I was just waiting for you to want to discuss it. Obviously, the two of you were very intimate at one time."

"Jean Claude came into my life at a very pivotal time. The people who raised me were calling me disrespectful of what they had given. My 'real' family had somehow gotten the notion that I wanted to leave them behind. Like I had any choice in the matter.

"I was nineteen, and he was a world traveler who was extremely generous and very married when we met. At least his wife was very married. He had the words and style to sweep me away from my little world.

'You are extremely bright.' he'd told me. 'Well-educated and most importantly, fiercely independent. I want you in my life forever.' He'd said this after the first dinner date I'd agreed to. He was very persistent but at the same time gentle and patient. I would not agree to become his mistress and live in the apartment he'd bought and furnished for me, but I did become his lover. Jean Claude justified the apartment to his wife as a place he needed in the city to entertain clients and display his works. He told her he didn't want to interrupt the flow of the family home with this business and as far as I know, she's never even bothered to see the place. It was a sweet situation for Jean Claude until he fucked it up, as least as it pertained to me.

"He taught me a great deal about myself and a most important lesson for which I am grateful. The more I found myself wanting from him, the more he would withdraw, telling me, 'Your first love should always be knowledge: your studies, your education. These things will be yours forever. No one can ever take away knowledge. And it will take you as far and high as you wish.' Whenever we made love, I always felt he was somewhere else. Do you know how it feels to be with someone and feel you are alone in the room? Well, that best sums up our relationship. But now I know it was nothing even close to love, not even a first love. You have shown me the difference."

"Yes Monique, I do know how it feels to be alone with someone's arms wrapped around you. Not a good place to be. Now I find myself smelling your fragrance when you are not even in sight. Even when I'm playing my guitar miles away from you, I can feel you wherever I may be.

"I wanted to ask you about the doorman's greeting when we walked into the building. But I was worried that since the interaction was obvious, I would come off as argumentative rather than just asking a simple question.

"Monique, you have me regretting all the time that passes between our being together. I have never felt this way about anyone ever before. Discovering more about one another should never be something we fear, but a way to make our relationship stronger. We've had many great months together here. My only concern is facing another brutally cold Quebec winter that I know is coming," Paul quipped in a joking but serious tone.

There were other things though. He was also thinking that Monique was such a cherished individual in her community. It often felt like both her female and male friends regarded Paul as an unworthy intruder. Paul had thought it would be easier to be introduced as an expatriate musician via Vancouver rather than someone who had willingly served as a soldier in Vietnam. Born and raised in the San Francisco Bay Area, just across from the home of the Black Panthers in Oakland California, he'd never had any interest in them. To Paul it was a simple conflict of basic philosophies. The Panthers proposed that all Whites were evil and all police were *Pigs*. He was raised to believe there were good and bad people in every group. This was not a very popular opinion within the young Intelligentsia Realm, so he had kept his thoughts to himself.

Even though they were all so protective of Monique, he felt no need to justify his presence or intentions regarding their relationship. On any given day, Paul could be asked how long he would be visiting Montreal and when he would be leaving. He frequently found himself at dinner parties and social functions being the only non French-speaking person. Even if there were other Black people enjoying the party, they too were fluent in French.

Apparently, many of the Black Canadians in Montreal were multigenerational. They were descendants of train employees, specifically the Pullman porters, descendants of runaway slaves, descendants of mixed race relationships who were identified as such by the color of their skin but not necessarily having the mindset, immigrants from the West Indies, from Haiti, and Africans from former French and British colonies.

In Canada, Montreal was second only to Toronto regarding ethnic diversity. But this included people of Chinese, Italian, Jewish, Irish, and Arab origins as well. When filling out official documents and the box 'Race' required a mark often 'Unknown' was checked.

Of course, those from mixed ethnic relationships were not always fully accepted by either group. They frequently complained that there was always some resistance from someone in the room. For those, it was easier to take the road of least resistance and either hookup someone with a similar circumstance to commiserate with, or marry and raise your children with the hope that they would find their identity with more ease and less conflict in a new and better world.

CHAPTER 23

PAUL ENROLLED IN AN ADULT NIGHT COURSE TO learn French, but had to quit after he found a gig that conflicted with his attendance. Musicians were as transient in Montreal as they were in Vancouver, so finding work had not been difficult. Monique was working as a teaching assistant while moving her way through the doctorate program.

Though busy, there was still time for fun. The Temptations were in town and Paul bought some tickets to celebrate Monique's birthday. He recalled the first time he'd seen the Temptations *live* at The Shrine Auditorium, 1967, in Los Angeles. It was a major stepping stone in his coming of age and cutting the proverbial cord. His mother had been adamant that he was too young to travel the four hundred miles south to Los Angeles with his cousin Jerry for the concert. But Paul remembered his counter-argument that people his age and just a year older were dying in Vietnam by the hundreds.

Ironically, a year and a half later, he would join that war voluntarily. He'd met so many interesting characters in those eighteen months in Southeast Asia and seen people die on both sides who didn't really deserve to die. But even when he'd quickly realized the futility of the situation, he'd still had to serve his enlistment time. He flashed back to being on life support. It had not been his plan to come that close loosing his life in a bug-infested jungle. His world for that time was kill or be killed and *surviving was the priority*.

But now here he was in Montreal, Quebec with a wonderful woman, feeling for the first time in a long time that his life was progressing. To where, he was still not sure. 'God bless the child that's got his own.' Yet he was turning twenty-five and was essentially living off another woman.

As winter approached again in the coldest place he had ever lived, Monique was very much back in stride with her academics - working as an Assistant Professor. As well, she was a busy guest lecturer at several University of Quebec campuses.

Her apartment was near the jazz club where Paul had found work. Through the autumn season he had continued jogging an average of four times a week. But as it became colder, he found himself finding more and more excuses not to run.

One day while running, Paul witnessed a young man on a bicycle being struck by a delivery truck. The contact threw the kid high into the air then tumbling several times over the asphalt street. It was a level of trauma he'd not seen since leaving Vietnam.

A bone in the young man's left leg, just under his kneecap, had torn through his pants and was sticking out. His right shoulder appeared to be out of its socket as well. Paul remembered many of his first aid tricks from Sgt. Harris and without a second thought or a moments hesitation he ran over to assist him.

A crowd had formed and someone had already gone to summon medical help. Paul bent over and reassured the guy. He calmed him down enough to be allowed to relocate the shoulder, and with a twist and pull of his ankle, he brought the broken bone back into place at the same time. Those watching began to cheer and applaud Paul for his quick response. A moment later, the paramedics arrived and rushed the man off to Montreal General Hospital close by on Cedar Avenue.

That night Paul made a decision to seriously consider going into the field of medicine, specifically, something to do with emergency work. This was an idea he'd had back in high school. He loved the adrenaline rush and the high when dealing with situations such as the one he had just experienced. There was *nothing equal*. During *the War* he'd had more than a few of these encounters and had found it easy to know just what to do while others were panicking and running away from the scene.

That night he surprised Monique with a fantastic dinner of shrimp and scallop sautéed with loads of butter, lemon, and garlic, served over pasta along with their favorite bottle of red wine. During dessert he shared with her the story of how he had helped the young cyclist. Monique listened to him intently. She soared with him, navigating a spiritual wind of enthusiasm she had always known was within him from the moment she'd first laid eyes on him. She followed his light brown eyes, sparkling so bright and radiant. Monique had experienced this feeling from him during their lovemaking, but it was so wonderful watching that level of emotional output from another context. *He had found what he was meant to do with his life.* She told him what she saw, but did not tell him she knew he would soon be leaving her.

Yes, Monique loved him but she also loved her life in Montréal as a Québécois and an educator, right where she was at exactly this moment. That night they embraced, kissed, and then melded together physically and spiritually. As she lay in his arms in the after warmth of their lovemaking, listening to Paul's sleep breathing, she indulged in one of her favorite pastimes. She recalled her memories of their time together chronologically, from the very first day until now. Each memory was like a pearl to be examined, touched, then strung back onto the necklace of their *Love*.

She wondered at how loving Paul and being loved by him had transformed her. After having experienced the betrayal of her birth parents and her adopted parents, the weakness of the father of her child, and the vulnerability of her circumstances, she had wrapped herself in a cloak of feminism for protection and survival. While she had saturated herself in feminism, she had completely missed the possibility of unconditional love. But now this man Paul had opened her heart to that elusive dream. Relaxing and settling into love took nothing away from the woman she had become. She was still a woman molded from lessons learned by her mistakes and reactions to life's setbacks, only now she felt more secure and clear than she had ever been. She knew her heart was safe.

She had everything she'd ever dreamed of already and there was still so much future ahead. Monique knew she was in a place in her life where Paul fit, but Paul had not yet figured out what he wanted from the world and what he had to give. He still had that look of a baby boy with a brand new toy even after all their time together. He was magnificent. His unique greatness was obvious to her, but not to himself.

Their time in Montreal and introducing Paul to her inner circle had not turned out as she had expected. Jean Claude and Rene enjoyed identifying *potential* in people who crossed their paths. They then used their wealth, status, knowledge, and wisdom to develop that quality. And they both gained great satisfaction and pleasure when *said people* reached their respective levels of success. Monique herself had been one of their projects and had felt their love and pride. But they showed no interest in Paul. She saw their indifference masked as cordial warmth. Why? Was it because he was not a Québécois against the French Establishment? That he was not from the West Indies? That he was not a pretty young woman?

Monique knew it was time for Paul to follow his destiny and she loved him well and enough to let him go. For a fleeting moment she allowed herself to imagine what it would be like to project their love, at this moment in time, to the ultimate height of what love could be. If they were to reconnect in the future, after he had accomplished his dreams, would they be able to reclaim this intensity and take each other to the end of love? The universe would determine that, she had to concede.

The flip side of the coin was what if he stayed and never realized his dreams? What then? Was his love for her deep enough that he could accept her success and good fortune while denying his own? Could he settle into being there for her, the reverse of what men commonly expected their woman to do? She then realized it was crucial to let Paul leave her, *to explore his potential unencumbered.* Their spiritual connection, their emotional connection she knew, would last forever. Reality in everyday life was much more complex.

Meanwhile, he was still with her now as she reached down and gently massaged between his legs. She got the exact and immediate response she expected and so continued their night of lovemaking. Such a wonderful thing, when two bodies truly meld together. Hearts beat in sequence, breathing in harmony, pleasure mounting to incredible heights with every touch.

The next morning as she stood in the kitchen, ready to pour the coffee Paul had just made, she told him he should pursue this gift of healing. Monique put her arms around him, gentle but tight. She moved her head against his chest so her ear pressed against his heart and whispered,

"Go. Do what you feel you have to do. Take your next step."

Within weeks he had packed up his things and travelled back to Vancouver. It was sincerely the toughest decision he had ever made. He had left JoAnn when he was conflicted by life and his identity. He had left Jennifer when he was confused by his actions, caught up in a life of submission to feeling good with no concern of tomorrow. In this instance, there was no conflict and no confusion. He loved this woman Monique. He loved her. But this was a power move for his future. Paul felt right about what he had decided to do and he would not fail. *Win or lose, he was going for the prize.*

He had to find something exclusive to him...something much more fulfilling than what he was doing. One thing he had definitely come to realize during his time with Monique was that her commitment to her studies and her life took a total effort. Their love was wonderful, but he envied the deepness of devotion she dedicated toward her intellectual pursuits. He would only be half a man if he could not meet her at the same level.

CHAPTER 24

BACK IN THE VANCOUVER AREA THREE WEEKS LATER, DJ rented him a room in his apartment which had been recently vacated when Rich had moved on to a doctorate program in psychology at the University of Southern California. The guys had upgraded to a two-bedroom unit since he'd last seen them.

Paul discussed his dream of making it into medical school with DJ, who was extremely supportive of his goal and offered to help in any way he could. DJ's current girlfriend, Sally, who was on the nursing staff at the Student Heath Center on campus, recommended that Paul take the Strong Vocational Test.

Whereas the vocational test he took for the Marines had pointed him towards the medical field, the results of this one showed Social Work or Chamber of Commerce Executive as most compatible with his skills. This was a total surprise. Both were acceptable careers, but he had been looking for reassurance that medicine was his calling in life. He'd scored considerably lower for the healing professions.

"You can't let some dime store test dictate who you are, Brotherman," declared DJ, "You gotta move in the direction your heart tells you. Why not sit in on a few classes and feed your mind on what's out there in the universe? Time will always be on your side. Allow for it to do its thing, Dig?"

Paul found the Simon Fraser campus to be very accommodating to folks sitting in on classes and even joining discussion groups. A very popular lecturer at the university was Professor William Dickson, head of the Business and Commerce Masters and Doctorate Programs. His presentation on the underutilization of the millions of brain cells we were born to master always drew standing room only audiences.

"Before those of you in the auditorium start concerning yourselves with anthropological nonsense of which race or species has the greater mind capacity, understand that Einstein only used eleven percent of his brain capacity. There is a lot of untapped brainpower in every person sitting in this room. And I qualified it to this room, because you ...by sitting in front of me today, have achieved the first step in expanding your power, by being here, seeking more."

After the lecture, Paul made it a goal to meet Dr. Dickson. DJ had told him that there was an open door policy at Simon Fraser University, which meant that the entire faculty made themselves available for drop-ins from interested students.

DJ had also told Paul that Professor Dickson was formerly the Dean of one of the University of Alaska campus'. Apparently he had chosen to leave that position and come to SFU where disenchanted U.S. educators made up a third of the faculty. Most had left the U.S. for political reasons as the War in Vietnam continued.

Professor Dickson granted him an appointment for the following week. All that was required was for the interested student to fill out a brief questionnaire about himself and the primary objective for the visit.

"I'm originally from Palo Alto," the Professor said, as he welcomed Paul into his office. "You left a scholarship at Stanford? What was that all about?" he asked in a very surprised tone of voice.

Paul was ready with an explanation. He had asked himself this same question a million times.

"I felt trapped in a world I needed to analyze objectively, from a distance. I was a spoiled brat who'd never realized how incredibly fortunate I was until I went to 'Nam. In my family everyone went to college and most became attorneys. Sounds naive, but I didn't even know there were adults who couldn't read or write. I thought those skills were like breathing in air or drinking water and though I knew an affluent life was not guaranteed, *I thought literacy was a birthright.*

"Yeah, I had thought the Watts riots and other racial conflicts were acts of social disorder from desperate people." Paul recalled the time a tape of one of Malcolm X's speeches had been shown in his high school civics class. "I remember being as frightened as my White classmates. 'The Revolution' would mean my family would be murdered as well, because we were part of the establishment. It was about *have nots* ending the reign of those who *have*. I sympathized with the poor and less fortunate, but could not see going against my own blood. So the side trip to the jungle with the U.S. Marines did serve its purpose, primarily thanks to my sergeant, Sgt. Harris. And the social and medical education I've experienced since leaving Stanford has placed me back in motion toward a defined goal. I know what I want."

Dr. Dickson was aware that Paul had been in Vietnam and told him that he was a veteran of World War II. He'd been assigned as the Commanding Officer of an all Black unit. It was covertly suggested that this assignment was punishment for him being in favor of integrating the Armed Forces, or in other words, being a Nigger Lover. But as he had expected, the Black soldiers were no different than the White soldiers, all just wanting to serve their country and get back home safe and intact.

The Professor had a way of asking questions that simply fell off his tongue. Talking to him was so conversational, like talking to an older friend. Then he blew Paul away with a compliment he was not expecting.

"It doesn't take any more than the time we've been talking to know that *You Are a Star*. You can be anything you set out to be, and I like the idea of you becoming a Doctor. But what you don't know, is you are *a marked man*. A big dark handsome guy like you will be despised by Whites and Blacks... who envy your good looks, your comfort with the English language. Most of the world can accept a Black person with street smarts, survival skills. But you readily come across as educated, intelligent, and comfortable within yourself.

"Remember this: you are *TOO BIG TO HIDE TOO DARK TO BLEND IN*, meaning always have your shit together. If you try to bullshit, you will be called on it. Those with power over you are just waiting for their turn to bring you down. And some will not even allow you to crawl away without inflicting as much strife as they can get in. By becoming a medical doctor, you will be your own man. You will control your own destiny.

"Another thing," Dr. Dickson said quietly, "do you have a special lady friend at this moment?"

"No, not exactly," answered Paul, but he hesitated. "I was recently involved in a relationship with a very dynamic woman in Montreal but we sort of broke it off, I guess, when I came back out here. I mean it wouldn't be fair to either of us to stay committed being across the country from one another."

"Well, remember this: you are in a serious stage of evolution right now. A trajectory of growth. A person you are involved with right now will probably not grow and change at the same pace. So there is a high probability that as you move forward on the *fast track*, she won't be able to keep up or for the matter, even realize she should."

Paul immediately flashed back to the life-sized photo of Monique at Jean Claude's apartment. Was Monique the exception or was she just exceptional?

"Don't fall in love at this time. You do not know who you will turn out to be. You will break her heart, or worse, blame her for not achieving your full potential. When you are truly pleased and satisfied you are moving in the direction you were meant to travel, that special person will come along. You will grow together.

"I have a daughter a year or so younger than you, and I would not like it if you fell in love with her at this time. Not because you are Black and she is White. But because you would likely break her heart, in spite of your best intentions. I would not want my baby to go through that. Of course, it would be her and your decision which direction your relationship would go. But you have such an enormous potential, chances are you would outgrow her and leave her behind.

"Think about it. Be upfront with your lady friends. I proposed to my wife two weeks after I met her; it worked out. We shared a wonderful life together until she died when our house burned down. No one can predict the future, but just think about what I am telling you. For right now, make your goal *to be all you can possibly be*. Then find someone to share it with."

Paul again flashed back to Monique. He'd been seriously feeling that he should have tried harder to make their relationship work. He knew he loved her, but he did not feel he was together enough to commit totally to anyone. Especially not to someone like Monique who really had a defined life and purpose. Dr. Dickson was Right On!

That was the first of many visits with Dr. Dickson. The Professor listened carefully to Paul's story about helping the injured young cyclist, and then called his golf buddy neighbor who just happened to be the Chief of the Orthopedic Department at Vancouver General Hospital. He in turn set Paul up with a job in the cast room, as an assistant. The pay wasn't much but the experience was invaluable.

The head orthopedic tech was a Black man named Quinn Bishop. They recognized each other immediately. "You were here before. Your friend had broken several bones in a motorcycle accident, Right? I remember Dr. Griffen and I set up the bed traction."

Paul recalled that night in Big Tom's room when Quinn had taken the time to shed light on their friend's situation and estimate how long he would be in the hospital. He remembered Quinn's kindness and consideration.

"You're American, right?" Without waiting for an answer, he carried on. "I was in the Korean War. Left Texas, came up here and married a Native American woman. Dude, we have seven kids, a new one every other year of our marriage. And don't buy the rumors you will hear that I have fathered several other children with women around the hospital."

Paul laughed to himself. He'd only just arrived and had already been told not only the rumor but specifically which women were involved: a nurse in the surgery department, a phlebotomy tech, and an emergency room physician who was one of the most powerful women on staff.

"Always put a little drop of food coloring in the water when you start making your cast, even for the older folks. It somehow makes a bad situation a little more manageable just by adding a little color to the standard white cast everyone else is wearing. I also find the kids tend to not rip them apart as fast."

Quinn instructed Paul every chance he got. "And another thing, in regard to the women you work with: keep your hands in your pocket and your dick out of their bellies. There are plenty of other ladies around town to enjoy. Trust me on that one, kid. I had to learn that the hard way."

The only issue with Quinn Bishop was his alcohol consumption. One never knew if his stories were real or fabricated. Paul had never fully understood the concept of a functional alcoholic, but now he did. Drinking and being competent in your job didn't seem to be compatible, but Mr. Bishop somehow seemed to manage the two quite well. The man was off the hook!

Quinn Bishop was a walking encyclopedia when it came to setting broken bones, converting hospital beds into traction units, and assisting the Orthopedic Doctors in surgery. He allowed Paul to hang out in the emergency department when they weren't busy. Paul was shown how to start IVs and the proper way to hold a needle holder to sew up minor lacerations. Because the place was busy and the doctors were understaffed, Paul was often assigned to patients who were so intoxicated or high that they didn't know if the person attending to them was a real doctor or not. But after several hours of waiting to be seen, they really didn't care.

In sharp contrast to the fine threads and expensive boots he'd worn onstage at Oil Can Harry's, Paul spent his workdays in sneakers, jeans, and a long white lab coat. If someone in the hospital recognized him from his musician days, they weren't letting on. Or was it just too far a stretch to imagine a person could go from being a nightclub entertainer to a hospital staffer? Whatever the reason, with the exception of

Bishop no one had verbally connected him to his past life. He liked that.

In the hospital, everyone had their assignment and functioned accordingly. After hours was a different matter but that was never allowed to interfere with the daily duties. Paul likened hospital life to an ant farm in a glass case he'd once had as a kid. He recalled seeing all the little tunnels and cells. There was always a constant stream of activity no matter the time of day. That's how Vancouver General looked.

Dr. Dickson had adopted him into his world. He invited him into his home to socialize with his family. He even gave Paul the use of his son's car, a VW bug, while the son was away for months at a time working on the Alaskan Pipeline.

Sailing with Doc Dickson was another wonderful experience. Doc said being on the water offered *a calm* like nowhere else. This was a feeling similar to what Paul felt when he was jogging, only better. No booze, no drugs, no music...only the sound of the wind, seagulls calling back and forth, and each other's voices. They talked about everything. Doc's boat was a thirty-six footer and he took it out every week. He taught Paul the nautical knots and how to follow the wind with the sails. Together they enjoyed sailing in and around the Strait of Georgia, English Bay, and Burrard Inlet. Although Paul was only able to get out six or so times, it was something he'd never forget.

CHAPTER 25

IT WAS A WHOLE NEW WORLD WHEN PAUL RETURNED to San Francisco. After Vietnam, Vancouver, Montreal, his hospital stint, and Dr. Dickson's rearrangement of his view on life in general, his confidence was soaring. Every encounter was another opportunity to make his mark. Whether it was to make a new friend, influence someone, or simply make another person smile, no matter the challenge, his only rule was *to do no harm*. He had left as a kid and returned as a Man.

"Dude, you really have changed," commented his Uncle Melvin as they sipped on a little blended Scotch. His uncle was now the pianist at the Mark Hopkins Hotel. He'd given Paul a membership to the Playboy Club in the North Beach as a welcome home gift.

The jazz scene was exploding all over town with The Blue Note in the Fillmore, Slim's on Divisadero; everywhere you turned a party was happening. It was the *Era of Feeling Good* and Marvin Gaye was the Grand Master. His music dictated the beat. But Paul was quick to realize this lifestyle was not for him. Uncle Melvin's life was enticing, just as his time in Vancouver with Steve and the guys had been, but now he was committed to keeping his focus.

Paul entered the Stanford undergraduate program through his GI benefits and a relatively new law passed in the late 1960s called Affirmative Action. This law was designed to counteract historic discrimination faced by ethnic minorities, women and other underrepresented groups. Paul was aware of the law, although he had never thought of himself as one of those people in need of government assistance. But Dr. Dickson had convinced him that this was the best way to get back into Stanford and once again, he was correct.

Dr. Dickson's generosity continued. He hooked Paul up with a friend of his who owned a college textbook publishing company. A job was offered. Paul felt that to return to college and be independent of his parents and the women he had been living with was *a must*. The job entailed cold calling professors around the Bay Area, introducing the textbooks the company had developed, and at the same time inviting the professors' input of ideas to improve the current textbooks in use in their classes. Often the company would help the professors develop their own textbooks to use in support of their curriculum.

Eighteen months in Vietnam, eight months on the West Coast of Canada, and ten months in Montreal was quite a lengthy hiatus from enrolment in a university. People were telling him his quest to be a doctor was near impossible. And the thought of getting up enough steam and vigor to compete with a bunch of kids for a seat in medical school was daunting. He was competing against kids who basically had stethoscopes thrown into their baby cribs and had been groomed to become doctors from that point on. Particularly the ones at Stanford now who were matriculating with those blinders well placed for winning the race to med school. Who would be crazy enough to think they could steal their seats?

However, Paul and Dr. Dickson had crafted a serious *game Plan*. Dr. Dickson was part of a higher education brain trust that helped construct programs designed for people like Paul. People with the potential to be gifted care providers and healers, but for whatever reason were not pre-med students. While they would still have to earn their BA or BS degrees with excellent grades, they would *not need pre-med* to be considered for medical school. So *the Plan* was to go back to Stanford because he'd already started a good track record there, and this time around take classes specifically intended to pad the GPA.

And that's exactly what he did. Paul achieved an A in Math 19, an A in Physics, and a B+ in Organic Chemistry. He chose psychology as his major and math as his minor. After getting his degree, the next step in *the game Plan* was to find a post-baccalaureate program and then onto medical school.

His new job with Clearworth Publishing Company was a dream position for someone wanting to get back into the college lifestyle and make not just good but *great* grades. He knew it would be a challenge to have a job while attending classes, but Mr. Lissey, Dr. Dickson's friend, was extremely helpful in adjusting Paul's work schedule to accommodate his school timetable. Talking with professors every day about their specific course needs and students helped Paul to understand the educational pursuit as a defined process.

And understanding the process led to understanding who the better grades went to, and why. Obtaining knowledge was the obvious goal of most students, but obtaining the desired high grade point average was a less understood process. Dr. Dickson had broken down another little gem for him: many times there is a very thin line between an A student and a B student. This didn't mean that much to the grader but it was a world of difference for the student. Always go for the A, expect the A, and let the grader know from the outset what your expectations are for that class.

Paul had found a little basement suite in San Bruno, close to the freeway. It was just adequate. After Jennifer's penthouse apartment and the dream relationship with Monique, he looked at his past life as a special gift that would be hard to match. But there were other blessings to come, he hoped. Meanwhile, he had to remain focused on his goal to become a doctor.

His parents were happy to see him back home and were very supportive of his plan to complete a degree at Stanford. He had thought about checking out JoAnn and talking about old times. She had just started law school and he'd heard through the grapevine that her marriage was OK, not great, but they were doing fine. Paul felt it best not to revisit that part of his past and besides, maybe her marriage was great. Maybe he was just being told what they thought he wanted to hear. But that was not the case; yesterday was yesterday.

Two years went by fast. Paul had accomplished phase one of *the Plan*. His spirits were further bolstered when he'd heard Sgt. Harris had managed to get the army to support his re entry into med school and was well on his way to becoming a doctor with a commitment to military services. Dr. Dickson had found out about Harris' good fortune and had passed this news on. Paul's communication with Dr. Dickson was ongoing and continued to be more than helpful to him.

Paul had received his BA from Stanford and had applied to several post-BAC programs, but so far had experienced no luck. Sunday morning basketball and jogging at least three times a week continued to be the primary constants in his life. Sitting in on an occasional jam session also happened, but not as often as he would have liked it to.

The week of graduation, Clearworth urgently needed an agent to cover the New Jersey and upper New York State territory. They promised a lot of cash and a possible promotion managing the Eastern Canada operation if all went well in New Jersey. It was also a chance to interview with medical schools on the East Coast.

He immediately thought of Monique coming back into his life. From their regular phone conversations, Paul knew she had completed her doctorate and was on track to becoming a top educator in her university community. They still loved each other and he completely embraced sharing her commitment to being a Quebecois. Paul had thought if the medical school dream did not materialize, learning French and living with her in Montreal was a viable alternative. "Sometimes it's not just all about you. Yeah, that's what love is. *Unity not Submission*," Paul concluded.

The only glitch was home base for Clearworth's Canadian branch would be in Toronto, so it was not a perfect situation, but still something to be considered.

Because of their busy schedules, Monique asked Paul if they could write to each other. She felt this would be more flexible and therefore more regular and personal than phone calls. More than once, she'd missed his call or had been just running out the door for an appointment and hadn't been able to talk. Paul found letter writing very difficult, in fact, he had previously found it impossible. But having learned the consequences of 'failure to communicate' from JoAnn and then Jennifer, he knew he had to try. Monique was that important to him.

Sometimes it's not just about you anymore, flashed through his brain again as he picked up the meditation beads she'd bought him on one of their excursions to Old Montreal.

After re-reading his first completed effort following several failed attempts, he was even more discouraged. His letter to Monique read like a report. Factual and accurate, but cold, stiff, and formal. Written words had always felt incomplete to him like he was missing something or not saying anything meaningful. On the other hand, what was put in writing could not be reversed or denied. What was this aversion to writing letters about?

'Great,' he thought 'another hard question.' He got up from his desk, walked over, slumped on the couch, and closed his eyes. Slowly, he remembered a time as a child when he'd over-heard his dad excitedly telling his partner about a letter that had turned up. Apparently, once it was introduced as evidence, their client's innocence would be proven. Maybe that was it. Maybe that's when he'd decided writing letters could be dicey.

Up until now, Paul's thoughts of Monique had fluctuated. Some days their time together seemed like a dream – a dream that was slipping away. Other times he wondered at how he had been able to leave her and felt physically ill at the thought. Yet other times he could smell her, taste her, feel her weight in his arms, and his body ached for her.

He imagined being surrounded by all those pillows on her bed with Monique curled at his side. Her head was on his chest and her hand was hypnotically tracing a simple pattern on his opposite shoulder. Over and over. How easy their talk was. No ego, no games, no insecurity. A heart-to-heart connection. Misunderstanding never lasted. Hurt feelings never happened. All it took was "Hey Wait, I thought...." *Honest communication and trust* kept their relationship alive and growing.

Paul opened his eyes, got up, and returned to his desk. Grabbing a fresh piece of paper, he started writing and this time the words seemed to flow off his pen. An hour later, he read over the four pages he'd written. They were filled with his current news, memories they'd made together, and a complete overview of all his thoughts and feelings in that moment. He knew she would love it. Actually, he was quite surprised to realize how much more he'd been able to express in written words than in his phone calls.

CHAPTER 26

SO PAUL PUNK'D OUT ON HIS RELATIVES A SECOND time. His parents had been planning a fantastic graduation party, a sort of makeup gift. But the latest job opportunity required him to work a few months in Michigan, starting immediately. *The Bookman* in Ann Arbor had had a family emergency and it seemed Paul was the only other Black guy in the company's sales force.

As civil unrest and mandatory curfews were a serious issue in places like Detroit and Newark, his being Black was a significant advantage for the company. The White guys feared the mob violence that was happening more and more frequently in the bigger cities all over America. As a Black Man, the threat was still there to a degree, but somewhat less. Still there 'cause it was also open season for law enforcement to express their pent up frustrations on 'them crazy Negroes and their White sympathizers.' Paul was one of only two Blacks in Clearworth's entire sales force. So they offered him *big* additional money, as an enticement to keep their inner city business alive.

On his arrival at La Guardia Airport Paul was met by Ray Smythe, the regional director for Clearworth. Ray was the first New Yorker he had ever met upclose and sort of personal.

A balding man in his early 40s, Ray reminded Paul of the Mad Hatter from Alice in Wonderland as, like the Hatter, he was blunt in speech and precise with his movements.

"Your plane was an hour late which has completely blown my schedule," Ray announced as he extended his hand for a quick shake. "I rented you a car and all you have to do is get to Interstate 95, it's the New Jersey Turnpike. Go to the New Brunswick area and rent a place. I put together some maps, your most important campuses to visit and a schedule. You did a great job in Michigan. You should have no problems here. Here's my phone number at the office. Oh, I guess you already have it. Well, here's my home phone if you can't get me at the first number. I live in Yonkers." And that was Ray.

Paul's territory in the San Francisco Bay Area had covered a 30-mile radius. It had increased to a 60-mile radius in Michigan and now, located in the middle of New Jersey, his territory encompassed over a 100-mile radius. It included three quarters of the State and ended just past New York's state capital, Albany, a 178-mile distance from what would be his new home base, the Rutgers University campus.

Driving the Interstate turnpike was awful…smoggy with horrible air quality from pollution bellowing from the industrial corridor of factories. It was so hot and humid. But when Paul got off of the turnpike and drove into New Brunswick, central New Jersey was actually quite rural. 'The Garden State' was pleasantly green for the most part, with a zillion little townships surrounded by trees of all varieties.

The Rutgers University campus was alive with students, activity and a personality of its own. Paul had taken to comparing and grading the campuses he visited. This was a little mind game he enjoyed. The University of Michigan was a much bigger place and had reminded Paul of the U of California, Berkeley campus. But Rutgers had more of an urban feel. Whereas McGill University blended into downtown Montreal, Rutgers seemed *to stake its claim* and create its own community. A river, the Raritan, was the dominant feature running alongside the northern side of the campus.

Paul had made it his custom to explore every campus he visited on foot…part of his *rate and compare game*. He often walked through the grounds and buildings for hours. Today after his tour he decided to hit the Busch Student Center. The plaque read "Charles L. Busch (1902-1971), formally known as 'University Heights Campus' this student center and dining hall is just one of his many gifts to our community." Paul found a seat and gobbled down a hamburger and some fries. He watched the students around him who were seemingly unaware of the world outside. *This* was their world.

Hunger satisfied, he found a billboard with a long list of apartments available for rent in and around the university. And he got lucky with the first place he visited, just across the Raritan in a place called Highland Park.

The Cohen family had converted a huge, Victorian style house into several units. Dr. Cohen had a local general medicine practice that his wife managed and their children were grown and lived elsewhere. Dr. and Mrs Cohen had built a newer, more modern home adjacent. Though they had a strict policy of renting only to Rutgers students, Paul convinced them he intended to eventually become a student. But right now his job required interacting with the faculty and so he needed to be situated close to the campus. Within a week, Paul was on the road cold calling faculty members throughout Central and Northern New Jersey. Ray had allowed him a few weeks to get settled before adding Upper New York State to his travel schedule.

On the day he moved in, Paul met a woman from the Graduate School of Education at Rutgers who lived in the apartment complex. Mary Lou Callahan's place was just above his apartment, which had formerly been the living room of the old house. Originally from Virginia, she was a tall, thin woman with a straight up and down athletic build. Her most attractive feature was her thick, naturally blonde hair.

They were cordial towards one another and often had conversations while sharing the outdoor space after the sun went down and the temperature cooled off. One day they talked about which professors Paul should call on to discuss his company's textbooks. She immediately recommended he visit the Reverend Doctor Samuel DeWitt Proctor. The man was working on his third doctorate degree at Rutgers and was an internationally known motivational speaker. On the work related side, Mary Lou thought that Dr. Proctor might be interested in putting together an advice manual for students considering the field of education.

But most importantly, she thought that Dr. Proctor might be the best possible person on the planet to help Paul figure out what he wanted to do with his life. She was not buying his current plan of moving to Canada and remaining in the textbook industry. So Paul shared with her his ultimate goal of attaining a medical degree. She was impressed that he had obtained his bachelor's degree from Stanford. Paul promised her he would make contact with *the right Reverend Professor* the moment his itinerary allowed him the time. He was certainly impressed with Dr. Proctor's credentials and accomplishments.

But his immediate concerns regarding the next step of *the Plan* were heightened by the multiple rejections to the post-BAC programs he'd recently applied to. He'd been granted interviews at the University of Michigan, Wayne State, and Michigan State. However, their programs all focused on minority students native to Michigan and particularly students with financial hardships. His being a veteran was a plus, but it seemed they were simply not interested. Their advice was to obtain a post-graduate degree in science or a pre-med program and then along with a top level Medical College Admission Test score apply to medical schools. In other words, follow the traditional road in...*not his Plan*. That road would take several more years...but he knew he was ready *now*.

What he didn't share with Mary Lou was that he was seriously thinking about a Plan B of becoming a college professor, perhaps in psychology. Or as a Plan C, he was considering maybe even going the route of Rich from Simon Fraser, who was now at USC and working his way towards becoming a motivational speaker. 'Perhaps Dr. Proctor could help in that endeavor,' he thought to himself. Paul had made several attempts to schedule appointments with Dr. Proctor, but for various reasons, something had always foiled their meeting. Then he was contacted by Dr. Proctor's office informing him that they would reschedule when there was an opening in the fall, as Dr. Proctor had now gone away for the summer.

Meanwhile, Clearworth was throwing lots of money his way. Unlimited expense accounts (as long as they came with receipts and proper documentation), making his own work schedule, and paid vacation time was not a bad way to go either.

One of his company's *connections* invited Paul to a party for the African American Association of College Professors. The event took place at one of the top restaurants in New York City, the Rainbow Room on the 65th floor of the Rockefeller Center. There were more than a few attractive Black women in attendance. 'So maybe it wasn't going to be an 'all about Business' evening after all.' thought Paul.

One of the foxiest ladies in the room was Grace Brockington. He recalled seeing her picture in the office of one of his professor clients in the psychology department at Rutgers, Dr. Charles Edwards. Paul had taken the liberty to inspect the photo with Professor Edwards who'd ignored the other seven or eight people in the picture and started proudly rapping about Grace. "She is my cousin. Her father is a prominent physician in Northern Jersey and one of the wealthier men in the State, Black or White period. Got lucky with some property developments owned by his family. You will find many Black families here in the North who were never slaves, or else they were granted freedom and bequeathed property from their owners. Grace and her brother have always been swimming in money. She really doesn't have to work, but after graduating from Fisk University, she lived in France for a while and learned to speak and write French fluently. She came back then earned her teaching degree from Seton Hall and now works part-time as a French teacher at a prestigious prep school. Part-time only, so not to interfere with jetting around to parties in DC, Miami, or other destinations."

Then Charles had looked closely at Paul. "You know, you kind of favor one of our relatives from Florida."

"Naw, Man. I don't think we have any kin folk in Florida, but I will check it out the next time I speak with my Mom," said Paul.

This conversation had taken place several weeks ago. Charles had been hooking Paul up righteously to the happenings around campus and had also introduced him to his Sunday morning basketball group. He had even introduced him to Paul Robeson, a popular alumnus of Rutgers. So when they saw each other at the party, they naturally started talking about a couple of the characters in the group.

Paul and Charles were laughing about an incident when he heard, "Mr. Marshall, I hear we may be related." Paul looked around to address the question being asked, and *lo and behold*, it was Grace Brockington.

Charles quickly introduced them formally to one another and then simply disappeared into the crowd.

"And what is your source of information?" he fired back.

"Charles had mentioned you would be attending this event today. He also said you are quite an exceptional basketball player. I love basketball. As a matter of fact, we have season tickets for the Knicks. So did you find out if we are related?"

"Yeah, I checked that out with my mom and she was aware of his people...er your family, but confirmed we weren't related."

"Even better. That means it won't be incest if I agreed to let you enter my secret garden," she smiled as she whispered into his ear for only him to hear. She began to walk away, then turned back and handed him a card with her phone number.

Paul tried to maintain every ounce of cool he could possibly muster as he stammered, "Dinner, next week?"

"OK. You're new to the East Coast, aren't you? So I will make a reservation at this cute little place that my cousin Charles turned me on to. It happens to be located in Highland Park."

"Wow, you really do your homework when seducing a guy, don't you?"

"Only if I feel it's going to be worth my time. I don't like being disappointed, on any level, so don't call it a seduction yet," she replied with a straight face, then a quick wink.

She was about five three and some change. She was wearing a pearl-covered sleeveless top and a short wraparound skirt that accentuated her legs - legs that could easily compete with Betty Grable's million dollar legs. And she was stacked with hips and lips…ravishing.

He hadn't allowed himself much female company while matriculating for his BA. Besides, Monique had set the bar so high that his interest just wasn't there. But Grace came on like a Mac truck and he was roadkill flattened by smokin' diesel tires.

Grace was *dangerous and exciting*: dangerous because she was the kind of woman who demanded a lot of attention and this required time his current work schedule didn't allow, and exciting because she was a challenge and he knew he would not disappoint her. She may be an international player, but he was willing to wager his last dollar that she had not met a Paul Marshall to date. The conquest would be a fun and different experience for him.

And so he began to accompany her and her friends to various outings and social events throughout the Jersey and New York area.

Both of them had been raised as part of the Talented Tenth community. In 1903, W.E.B. Dubois had developed the theory that the Negro race, 'will be saved from within by its exceptional men.' To overcome the problem of substandard education among Negroes, the Talented Tenth evolved to establish and maintain educational institutions of high standards to overcome the fact that most colleges at the time would not accept Blacks.

Paul and this young lady, Grace had both enjoyed the company of other privileged Black children in Jack and Jill organizations around the country. The programs had included attending the annual meetings of the NAACP, whose purpose was 'to ensure the political, educational, social, and economic equality of rights of all persons and to eliminate racial hatred.'

The problem that Paul had with upper crust organizations such as the Talented Tenth, especially now in the 1970s, was that all too often, they seemed like a caste system. The goals and organizations they created to fight racism discriminated against their own. Those Blacks who didn't have the cultural ways and means to emulate White Society were blocked from joining the *clubs* that had been created. With this mandate for admission, these organizations seemed to have lost their Black identity.

Where were the breakfast and lunch centers that the Black Muslims and Panthers had established in their communities? Where were the NAACP-funded Health Clinics and Shelters built by Elijah Muhammad and his followers? 'Learning to talk White and act White would make everything right' was their modus operandi. The Talented Tenth were identifying with the Oppressor not the Oppressed. They were truly Frantz Fanon's Black Skin White Mask characters.

It hadn't seem wrong when he was growing up, but Paul had come to understand that this way of thinking was exclusionary to the rest of the Black race.

Paul had sat in on one of Monique's lectures on the Hindu caste system. The system was defined in the Hindu Holy Book, the Vedas and these scriptures guided Hindus in their daily life. There are some 3,000 castes subdivided into 25,000 sub-castes. For example, a train porter would be of a higher sub-caste than a truck driver who would therefore not be good enough to marry the porter's daughter. The castes or *jati* - which means race in most Indian languages - are grouped into four categories called *varna* which means color. In other words, the lighter the color, the higher the varna.

The caste system reminded Paul of the Brown Paper Bag rule in the South: if a person was darker than the bag they were *not invited to the party*.

He knew racism was a world problem, but racism against Blacks in America went even further. It was about the *slavery legacy* of being subhuman and property only. The inequities in education standards he'd first become aware of in Vietnam and the inequities in the health care system he'd recently observed while volunteering at the clinic in New Brunswick were *purposefully contrived*.

His volunteerism was part of *The Plan* to better his profile for entrance into medical school, but it had a surprising benefit, an epiphany even. Becoming a doctor was more than just acquiring a title. It was *a means* to helping the community, as a whole, in a very direct manner. He truly saw the need for more Black doctors. Many of the children and adults who came to the clinic had never seen a Black doctor. When Paul thought back to growing up in California, he could only recall two or three himself.

Maybe Doc Dickson knew he would come to this realization sooner or later. Maybe Plan B or Plan C for his future were not viable alternatives after all. His commitment needed to be to medicine.

Now Paul found himself infatuated with a young woman who reminded him of many of the people he had grown up with in San Francisco. They too were from upper middle class Black families. Before meeting JoAnn and becoming familiar with her more accepting and quieter explanations of their behaviour, he could not tolerate the constant bickering and bourgeois ways of this crowd. And now here was Grace, at the top of the heap, with her father being touted as the richest Black man in New Jersey. Infatuation was a good word to describe his interest in Grace, or maybe this was his fascination with 'danger and excitement.'

Grace endorsed Paul becoming a college professor, and was even willing to look past his darker complexion. Both of her parents were very fair complexioned and her mother had subjected Grace to many conversations regarding her desire for light-skinned grandchildren. Surprisingly, Grace was willing to ignore the complexion thing, but told him explicitly that if he chose to become a physician, they could not have a serious relationship or a future.

It seemed her mother, who had been a nurse when she met her father, had sacrificed her career in order for his to succeed. But instead of being able to enjoy their life together, she'd essentially lost him to his patients and the practice of medicine. This often told story about her father not being around for his wife or his children but always being available for his patients and the hospitals' needs was something Grace's mom was never going to let go.

Grace's statement of 'not liking to be disappointed' was apparently deeply rooted in her upbringing. Consequently, after several months of pursuing a relationship with Grace, he was moving away from the idea of becoming a doctor. Not to mention her cousins connections at Rutgers would be a huge asset if he were to choose an academic career. But deep down inside he felt ending up with a person like Grace would be backsliding into the world of JoAnn. If living in Canada had taught him anything it was that power came from knowing oneself, not from association with the so-called elite.

While accompanying Grace to another fabulous, upscale party in Manhattan one Sunday, Paul found himself engaged in a conversation with a gentleman who practiced orthopedic surgery. The man was as disinterested in the goings-on of the party as Paul was.

Dr. Percival Washington and Paul found they had several things in common. The doctor had served in Vietnam in the earlier stages of the War and had also lived in Montreal for a time where he had completed a Sports Medicine Residency at the Royal Victorian Hospital. Montreal had just been awarded the 1976 Summer Games, and he'd been invited to be part of the medical team they were putting together.

"So this Book Gig," the Doctor asked, "is it truly floating your boat?"

"Absolutely Not!" Paul replied with vigor. He then ran down his plans of getting into med school and becoming a trauma surgeon.

"Well, consider orthopedics as well. After the time you spent at Vancouver General, you would have an inside track on doing well. Also, having been an athlete and a musician, you have an innate feel and higher appreciation for human performance on both a physical and spiritual level. Keep those muscles and joints not just working, but *singing* as well. And what's more important?" Dr. Washington said proudly.

He continued, "In Health Care, dealing with diabetes and cancer is important, but setting them bones right can be just as important to the overall wellbeing of a community. Racism is everywhere, certainly in healthcare. And we all need to be vigilant in fighting it however we can."

The drive back to New Jersey that night was like riding a wave. Everything they passed on the road was a blur as Paul rolled the conversation around in his mind. Grace chose to sleep, as was her habit when travelling by car regardless if it was a long or a short drive.

"I heard parts of your conversation with Percy," Grace stated as the car came to a stop at her apartment in Somerset. "So you're still headed in that direction?"

"Maybe," Paul replied. "I'm keeping all doors open."

"Well, remember what I told you awhile ago. If you move in that direction it will be in serious conflict with my being part of it. Don't bother coming up tonight; I've got a migraine."

When he arrived back at his place, Paul found a message on the door left by Mary Lou.

Dr. Proctor would be available to see him tomorrow.

CHAPTER 27

PAUL HAD DONE A LITTLE RESEARCH ON DR. Proctor. It was routine procedure to find out as many details as possible before alerting the company regarding a potential new author.

Samuel Proctor had established himself as a preeminent theologian, orator and educator throughout the country. He was a Professor Emeritus at Rutgers University and Pastor Emeritus of the Abyssinian Baptist Church in Harlem. He'd earned a doctorate in theology from Boston University and then became president of two colleges: Virginia Union, his alma mater; and North Carolina A&T. He'd served as associate director of the Peace Corps under Presidents Kennedy and Johnson. A speechwriter for Hubert Humphreys presidential campaign of 1968, he was also the Associate General Secretary of the National Council of Churches and headed the Institute for Services to Education. And, according to Paul's neighbor, Dr. Proctor was responsible for turning around the lives of literally thousands of students and young people including Mary Lou, who had sat in on his presentations of *Achievements on a Personal Level*.

The next day, Paul arrived at Dr. Proctor's office early. As he sat there waiting, he watched two students entering then leaving the office, back-to-back, distraught and disappointed. By the time it was his turn, he'd resolved that he would propose the idea of Dr. Proctor developing a book deal on education and leave his own personal matters regarding med school for another day.

As he started his pitch and proceeded to introduce the company to the Professor, he felt as if he had been thrown under a microscope. The man gave off an air of incredible insight and presence. Paul briefly flashed back to his first encounter with Dr. Dickson. It was amazing how these two powerful men from very different worlds seemed to have such similar mannerisms. For example, the way they were able to conduct an interview that had him addressing topics that seemingly had no relevance *to anything*. But after reflection, he realized it was brilliant as to how much information these answered questions provided. He asked where Paul had been born and where his parents lived. Not asked what they did for a living, just where were they living, and were they still together? The answers revealed whether he was from a single parent family and gave a snapshot of his upbringing. Was he married? An opening for how a person felt about relationships, commitment, or for that matter, distractions. Where did he go to school? Did he play sports? How did he get this job? Was this his future? What would he rather be doing?

Paul had been giving safe answers until he became frustrated. He'd tried to stay with his plan of sticking to the book business, without success. Dr. Proctor had dismantled his invisible shield quickly.

"If you must know, I want to be a trauma surgeon, maybe even an orthopedic surgeon. What can you do about it?"

"I'm not sure yet," Dr. Proctor responded calmly, "but you don't look like a salesman to me. Maybe we can get you off this book route and on your way to medical school. What were your grades like in science?"

Paul was floored. The moment he had been waiting for was before him. *Here and Now.* He was talking about med school with a very influential man!

Apparently, two days ago the Professor had attended a dinner at the home of Dean Logan. Dr. Logan was the only

Black Dean on the medical admissions board of The College of Medicine and Dentistry of New Jersey Piscataway Campus. The conversation that night had been about putting together a plan to find medical students who would bring a different frame of reference to the field of medicine - students who would think *outside the box* more so than the usual pre-med applicants. For the first time ever, applicants without a strictly biology or chemistry background *would be considered*, thus creating a more open attitude to practicing medicine.

Paul flashed on *timing is everything* then *being in the right place at the right time*. It was now or never. The interview was live with no retakes. A sudden thrill arose from deep within his gut. It felt good.

The immediate plan for change was to accept more women and minorities into med school. So Paul's first step was to meet Dr. Logan. But after several attempts to meet with the Dean, for whatever reason, he was never available. Paul had left all his personal info and had not heard back. This did not surprise him as his CV was not studded with all A's nor were there any stellar letters from class professors.

Becoming impatient and frustrated with *in limbo*, Paul decided to use his book salesman skills and go directly to the Dean of Admissions office with the hope of talking to someone with a connection to the selection committee.

When he arrived at the office, Paul looked around and saw a dude with the nameplate 'Myron Garvin' on his desk. The guy looked very approachable and was the only other Black person there. Paul decided to be direct. He introduced himself then told how he had met Dr. Proctor and was interested in being admitted to their medical school.

"Very interesting." said Myron. He then told Paul to follow and walked him straight into the office of Dean Mason. The Dean of freaking Admissions - the *Main Man*.

Whereas Dean Logan sat on the committee, *this* was the man with the final say. Paul had hoped to get close to a decision-maker but had never expected to get here!

'Hey Baby, its game time once again' popped into his head. Paul hadn't had this feeling since his team had made their run for the State Championship his senior year in high school.

He'd set a record still standing for the State, 40 consecutive free throws without a miss. Was remembering this now a good omen?

Dean Mason was about six foot three, mid-fifties. Paul had become good at sizing up peoples' ages and their position in the pecking order, and this guy was clearly at the top of his game. The man wore a well-manicured beard and had a belly that extended past his belt. Sitting on his desk was a rack of pipes that appeared to be a collection from different parts of the world. He obviously loved good food and smoking his pipe.

Myron Garvin gave Dr. Mason a sly grin and said, "Mr. Marshall comes directly from Dr. Proctor's office. He was told that Dr. Logan was the key to him getting into Rutgers Medical School. The Brother somehow feels that you may be of some assistance, as Dean Logan has not been available to meet with him. I told him that *possibly* you could be of assistance." The two of them were obviously sharing some humor.

Dean Mason smiled and removed the pipe he was smoking from his mouth. It seemed like everything was in slow motion as he went for another one on the rack and replenished it with a different blend of tobacco. He then sat down, not behind his desk but in one of the two chairs standing on the Persian carpet, and invited Paul to take the other. He was extremely cordial as he listened to Paul's story. After a long silence, he replied, "Dr. Proctor has never sent us a bad apple yet...Leave your resume and CV and I will pass it on to our Admissions Committee."

Paul, feeling that leaving his papers had not worked in getting to Dr. Logan, was reluctant to risk having this *once-in-a-lifetime opportunity* end with the same frustration. He felt he just could not leave this office without a stronger reassurance.

"Dean Mason, I am presently working for a company based in California. I'm not trying to jive you; I'm not from the ghetto nor have I been convicted of anything. I've been told *I am a Star* by two different men for whom I have the utmost respect. And now, I have a one-in-a-million chance to make my dream come true...to *Become a Doctor*.

"I'm ready now. I know you can't pass my test or knight me with a magic sword into medicine. If I get accepted into your post-BAC program, I'll have to quit an extremely well paying job and will have no financial support going forward. I know you can't guarantee me anything, but Dr. Proctor believes in me and I know I will make an excellent doctor one day... however, I really need some help right now. I have to find a job and do whatever is necessary to make this happen."

Dean Mason listened again, began stroking his beard, smiled, and said, "Well, uh, Paul is it?" Paul confirmed his name. "Come back in a couple of days and we'll see if we can work something out."

Two days later, Paul returned. Dean Mason and Myron Garvin had checked him out thoroughly including calls to everyone from Dr. Proctor to his landlords. They'd reviewed letters of support from his professors at Stanford, Dr. Dickson, and even his Commanding Officer in Vietnam, all within 48 hours.

"I have decided to put you into our summer program with several other candidates we are hoping will do well and win one of the 100 seats available for next year's Medical School Class. I noticed you completed your major in psychology...do you have any interest in Psychiatry?" Dean Mason asked.

It took Paul only a second to respond, very enthusiastically, that Psychiatry was a consideration. Dean Mason then arranged an informal get together with the Chairman of the psychiatry department in his home for the following night.

By the end of the evening, it was arranged that Paul would move into the newly built Acute Psychiatric Building at the Medical School. His living quarters would be adjacent to the locked ward and his duties as an attendant would include administering medications to the inpatients and assisting in several studies that Dr. Robbins, the Program Director and personal friend of Dr. Mason, was running.

He let his landlords know that he simply could not afford to stay where he'd been living. The company did not take his resignation well, and Grace simply stopped taking his phone calls.

He enrolled at the community college to take the couple of courses that Dean Mason and Myron Garvin felt were important to have under his belt before the summer program at Rutgers began.

Paul aced the college courses and the summer program unfolded wonderfully.

Skipping the post-BAC Program, Paul was admitted to the University of New Jersey at Piscataway or simply Rutgers Medical School six months after leaving Dr. Proctor's office.

CHAPTER 28

AN EARLY LESSON FROM HIS FATHER PERTAINING TO the field of law was to realize that the legal profession is essentially a *fraternal brotherhood* that requires a skillful process of communication to succeed. It was not necessarily about which law had been broken or violated but more about how the facts were presented to the judge.

'In fact,' Paul thought, 'all fraternal organizations worked the same way.' The field of medicine certainly was no different. It was also a fraternal brotherhood primarily using Latin-based phraseology to communicate the facts to one another.

What was not expected but understandable he thought, especially if you'd played sports on a competitive level, was that folks can be very cut throat at times. Not all his class-mates were like that, but enough that he learned to keep his guard up at all times. For instance, if an assignment required a trip to the library, sometimes the most pertinent page was torn from the book, or occasionally, the entire book was missing from the shelf.

Paul found himself on several occasions recalling Sgt. Harris' med school nightmare of the lab instructor who had accused him of cheating because he'd been jealous of Harris' blossoming friendship with a fellow female student.

Apparently, this instructor was romantically interested in the young lady himself. And ultimately, this was the action that led to the physical altercation that was Harris' undoing.

Lab instructors were the unseen controllers in many situations. They were often the difference between passing or failing a particular assignment, and unlike the Professors, they frequently fraternized with the students on a more intimate level that everyone accepted as commonplace. Dealing with them on both levels was a tricky and treacherous process. But Dr. Dickson had turned Paul on to the value of developing better people skills and not underestimating anyone because they seemed to be of minor importance. So he was prepared.

The amount of material expected to be mastered in a short amount of time was the scary part.

Fortunately, putting in the extra time and effort to accomplish his goals had long ago become second nature to Paul. His coaches, from sandlot baseball through to Pop Warner's football and then his music teacher in high school, deserved a lot of the credit for his discipline and work ethic. Also he had to include his nine years of parochial school and the nuns. And of course, the U.S. Marines. All had contributed to his determination to succeed.

One day while on the Pediatric Service at Muhlenberg Hospital, Paul and his group of medical students followed the attending pediatrician, Dr. Patricia Millar, to the emergency department to evaluate a little boy with a fractured leg. Dr. Millar first took the students to the gurney the child was lying on. The leg was swollen and looked hot and angry but the child just laid there motionless and somewhat detached. The X-rays were up on the view box. Dr. Millar asked the students to describe what they were seeing there.

As usual, Roger Goldstein, the class' self-appointed superstar, spoke up first: "There is a fracture of the tibia, oblique and non-displaced. It should heal without any problems."

"Mr. Marshall, do you agree?" the Attending asked.

Paul looked closely at the films and observed other deformities. In particular, he noticed what appeared to be a healed fracture above the new break and another near or just above the child's ankle. He had recalled a similar case while working with Quinn Bishop at Vancouver General. He pointed out his findings to his Professor and classmates.

"Precisely. This child was here several months ago with a fracture of the same leg. I'm concerned that this might be a case of child abuse. I have already notified Social Services. Good work, Mr. Marshall."

Paul felt the same inner pride he had felt before in Montreal when dealing with the injured cyclist. This feeling reaffirmed to him that *his life was most definitely moving in the right direction*.

Then one day the wheels threatened to fall off the wagon, when Paul was summoned to Dean Mason's office.

CHAPTER 29

"WE HAVE A SERIOUS PROBLEM. AS YOU KNOW, AT the end of this second year at Rutgers your class will receive a Masters of Medical Science and half of your classmates will have to complete their third and fourth years at other medical schools."

The Dean paused to refill the bowl of his pipe. Paul had become familiar with this being a common move when Dr. Mason was searching deeper for the right words.

"You are familiar with Doctor Polinski, the head of the Pathology Department? Yes, Well, she also sits on the admissions committee and is a very outspoken person. For some reason she has taken a stand against your being admitted into our third year program."

Paul was flabbergasted. Of all his professors, he thought she and he had shared an excellent level of communication. In fact, she was from Montreal and had invited him to several functions off-campus along with some other classmates. He'd passed on a couple of her events but it was for academic reasons. He thought she had admired him for his dedication to his studies, rather than taking offense.

"Really, Dean Mason? I can't think of any reason why she would be a negative vote. I thought she knew how much I want to stay at Rutgers. I cannot imagine what I said or did for her to be against me."

"Well Paul, it's not that she questions your interest in becoming a doctor; she questions your overall motives. You see, somewhere she has formed the opinion that you are more interested in driving a Big Red Cadillac and strutting around the Black community than wanting to help your people from a medical standpoint. Can you think of where she came up with this image of you?" Paul remained speechless.

"As you know Paul," he continued, "you and the nine other minority students we chose for your class were selected primarily on the basis of your perceived interest in giving back to your communities and making a profound difference in the quality of their health care.

"We have gotten to know one another fairly well. I like that you have continued to volunteer at that health clinic in New Brunswick that Myron started five years ago. It's primarily dependant on medical students' participation and we will be incorporating it into the curriculum hopefully in a year or two. Mr. Garvin joined our administrative staff as part of the Community Outreach Program. If he plays his cards right, he has a good chance to be admitted to our post-BAC program then onto med school himself.

"And how have you found the time to be in the Mentor Project for Dr. Proctor's undergrads committed to getting a degree? A smart move on your part, *giving back* for Dr. Proctor's generosity to you. You're a solid guy, in my book. You would not have been admitted if there was any doubt that you couldn't graduate.

"But Dr. Polinski seems to be basing her opinions on an encounter she had with you *before* you came to Rutgers! She told me that at first she wasn't sure. But when she recalled where she had met you before and tried to get to know you better in order to overcome her suspicions, you seem to side-step or straight up ignore her overtures. So she assumed that you were aware of that previous encounter and thought it could be swept under the carpet. What in the world could she be thinking about?"

Paul went deep into thought and immediately felt a sense of defeat. He thought back to his initial reservation in believing Sgt. Harris when he had told Paul how he got kicked out of medical school. Was *he* now facing the same fate?

Just then he remembered a conversation with Doctor Polinski where she'd recalled watching a guy who looked a lot like him at a Temptations Concert back in Montreal. Paul had laughed it off as 'it must have been someone else.' On the one hand her questions seemed playful and no big issue, but on the other hand he felt like there was another agenda. Once again he'd felt like he was being put under a microscope.

With Dr. Proctor, it was obvious probing, but there was a *building up* at the same time, by talking about his leather briefcase and how stylish his suit and shoes looked. Dr. Proctor's motivation had purely been *fact finding* in the shortest time possible.

Dr. Polinski, on the other hand, was looking for holes in his style, his presentation. Damn, if you look hard enough at anything, you can always find flaws. Why submit yourself to a smackdown if you don't have to? This had always been Paul's philosophy. So maybe he *had* subconsciously, avoided her since that night.

Then he remembered another encounter at one of the first Meet the Faculty evenings the medical school had organized as a social between students and their professors and lab instructors. Paul recalled how she had cornered him at the punch bowl and went into this long-winded speech. 'Only the best of the best deserved to be in Medical School, only thoroughbreds belonged. The children of other doctors or those who were the top students of their pre-med classes ready to create a path for breeding babies of their own who would become doctors.' At the time, Paul didn't know if he was being ostracized or challenged on lack of pedigree, but he was definitely turned off by the conversation. Here was another reason he'd avoided speaking to or becoming further acquainted with the professor.

Suddenly, Paul put the pieces together and said, "You know Dean Mason, several years ago when I was living in Montreal, I took my girl, Monique, to a Temptations Concert. A very good friend of hers had organized a little get together. Jessica was in the theatre business and loved theme parties. And as her birthday gift to Monique, she wanted all the friends to dress up and have dinner together before the concert. Jessica's company was staging *Guys and Dolls* at the time and she had created all the costumes for the show. So she arranged for everyone to borrow outfits from the production. I dressed up in this bright red suit with a matching fedora as 'Nathan Detroit' and Monique dressed up as his Lady, 'a Showgirl' dreaming of the straight and narrow. And she really got into it. She walked around wearing cheap perfume and smacking Doublemint gum in a slinky little dress with a wig and hat to disguise herself.

"Dr. Polinski swore she saw me that night. I thought I'd done a good job of dismissing it from her mind. Guess I didn't. I was dressed as a con artist and Monique.... Well, the picture must have stuck."

Dean Mason had never laughed so hard in Paul's presence. "Well, Young Man, somehow you have got to convince her that you were not a pimp or a con man in Montreal! I know that your goal for becoming a doctor is not to buy a fancy car and only heal your pocketbook! I know the house you were raised in. But Dr. Polinski thinks you're a hood rat, from the ghetto.

"I'm not suggesting that a kid who's been dealt a tough hand at birth can't become a doctor and contribute to his community, but Dr. Polinski has said some pretty incredible, racist things about people not being able to escape their roots. Dr. Proctor and I never believed that crap. Everyone deserves a chance to reach their full potential.

"You were blessed with a great family and all the opportunities in the world to become whatever you wanted to accomplish. You just got a little sidetracked.

"Of course, you can't let Dr. Polinski know we've discussed something that came up in our Admission Committee Meeting. But you can fix this thing, Kid. Only you can fix this."

Paul thought long and hard regarding how he was going to change her vote.

To think it wasn't just about doing well in the classroom was a shocker. But even more so, to be dismissed because she felt he was a lesser person from lower stock *just wasn't fair or right*. A school concerned that the moral component of their 'physician product' was as important as the book learning, was a good thing. But to be judged or pigeonholed before having a chance to overcome a stereotype???

This was information he planned on sharing someday with kids being blocked from succeeding in their life's goal, whatever it may be. But in this moment, Paul knew he *belonged where he was right now*. He felt it with every fiber of his being.

CHAPTER 30

PAUL RECALLED THAT HIS PATHOLOGY PROFESSOR always passed through the school cafeteria for a coffee on Tuesdays before her eight o'clock lecture. The only possible chance he had to convey his commitment to medicine was by somehow showing her he was a truly humble, hard working student. One who was willing to put in as many hours as necessary to get the assignment completed.

He'd stayed up all night studying. His eyes were blood red; his afro was intentionally uncombed. He sat close to the door she would pass through on her way out of the cafeteria.

"Paul, is that you?" she called out with sincere astonishment.

"Oh, hi Dr. Polinski," Paul said, barely raising his head.

"Have you been here all night?"

"Well, not in this chair but...you know, I've been thinking long and hard about something you mentioned to us after one of our classes. You spoke about the time and effort it will take to truly become an excellent physician. And that's the kind of doctor I want to be, not only for my patients but for myself as well. Here I am studying just to pass a test, but to think this extra effort may save someone's life one day...well it's an amazing thought, and scary at the same time!"

When Paul looked up, he was floored to see tears streaming down her face.

"You know, Paul, I was worried that you had not grasped the concept that what we're doing here is all-encompassing, *a total package*. It gives my heart such a lift to hear you say those words and know you understand." And without further words, she left.

Two days later Paul ran into Dean Mason. "I don't know how you did it, Kid, but Doctor Polinski did everything short of cartwheels getting you accepted for your final years at Rutgers. Congratulations!"

'This is the best news ever!' Paul thought to himself, and even better was that it wasn't an act. He believed every word he had told Doctor Polinski. There is *no place for holding back* when winning is on the line or you're at risk of losing a great opportunity before you.

The moment Paul received his letter of acceptance along with his Clinical Rotation for the upcoming year was wonderful. The early morning was still cool with the promise of the heat to come as he stepped outside. The fragrance of honeysuckle was strong that morning. Paul sat down on one of the chairs in his backyard with a view of the river and the Rutgers Campus on the other side. "This is what I will see for the next two years as a medical student," he whispered outloud. He knew it had come about solely through blind faith, along with believing in himself and somehow knowing the universe was moving him in a direction that was meant to come together just the way it had.

He thought back to what he'd learned as a musician. Not to underestimate *the power* of getting into the flow of the music. His medical books had a flow too, interwining information with reasoning.

Jimi Hendrix had so much more to offer the world with his talent. He understood so well the rhyme and reason of his music. And he gave his all, his abundant God-given talent. But he let drugs take him *out*.

The Beatles wrote: *and in the end the love you take is equal to the love you make* and knowing these words to be true was another valuable lesson of life he had come to understand.

Monique had truly breathed life into those words, and he hoped he would find his way back into her life one day. Then and there he decided she'd be the first person he'd invite to his graduation, two years from now.

Then he wondered if he would always use music to reference what was going on in his life. 'Probably,' he thought. As Richie Havens had told him, music was the Universal Communicator.

Paul's thought train rolled on to Doc Dickson making him understand his physical presence was *Too Big to Hide and Too Dark to Blend*. Therefore, he knew he would always be called on, whether in class, at work, *wherever*. He must always be prepared to explain what was in front of him. Know your worth, but stay focused on the task at hand, and think before speaking. Bullshit may get you over, but owning knowledge should always be your goal.

You may be perceived as a jive talker based on a previous experience a person may have had with people of color. Don't let their stereotype thinking, their lazy mentality, define who you are. They may give you a degree in street smarts initially, but always leave them knowing you have read and understood the book.

Paul knew there was no substitute for capturing the essence of what was being studied and being able to explain the subject completely. His medical professors had always stressed that the subject was not learned until you could explain it to the Chief of Staff and, just as well, to a patient with a third grade education.

Paul now knew that standing out in a crowd because of the color of his skin or the size of his person meant immediate recognition. He would look at it as an opportunity to excel, to impress, and to enlighten with his personality and intelligence. 'Thank you, Dr. Dickson, for making me aware of who I am and seeing my physicality as a gift, not a burden.'

The thought expanded for Paul. 'Thank you Sgt. Harris for making my military stint something that contributed to my growth as a human being, as a proud Black Man, being comfortable with the face I see in the mirror.

'Thank you Dean Mason. For being there for so many people like myself who may have never had the chance to contribute to medicine without your courage to go to bat for those of us without the traditional prerequisites. Thank you for recognizing we too deserved a chance to succeed and achieve.

'Thank you Dr. Proctor for including me in erasing the stereotype, reversing the bad data, and securing a higher level in our society that we may never have achieved without your insight and encouragement.

To these *Mentors*, gratitude almost wasn't enough. Parents develop our confidence and self-worth by affirming how special we are. But having men at a high level of expertise with such wisdom tell us we are special is *a powerful thing that makes all things seem possible.*

In his awareness of all these valuable gifts, Paul was filled with gratitude for their contributions. But when all was said and done, Paul knew that *he, himself* had accomplished this.

CPSIA information can be obtained
at www.ICGtesting.com
Printed in the USA
FSOW01n2056150617
35286FS